~~Crossing~~ Croissant THE CHANNEL

NEXT STOP, FRANCE

BY

PETER HANRAHAN

ILLUSTRATED BY DANDI PALMER

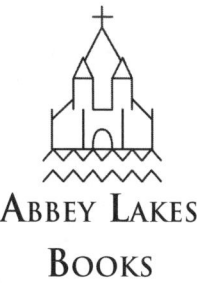

ABBEY LAKES
BOOKS

British Library Cataloguing in Publication Data
A catalogue record for this book is available from the
British Library

ISBN 0-9548374-0-1

Typeset by Amolibros, Milverton, Somerset
This book production has been managed by Amolibros
Printed and bound by T J International Ltd, Padstow, Cornwall, UK

Many thanks to Keith, George, Christie and Joseph for their contributions. And to Rachel who in between giving birth kept the whole thing going. Especially to Sue for her encouragement, support, and hard work. Of course to Linda and the children, James, John-Mark and Philip (who paid me to be included in the acknowledgments). To Jane for all her efforts. Ryan, Suzanne and all the family and friends who have done their bit. My mother and father, Aunty Frances...

Chapter One

Denis Wilson was a Francophile and if that meant being named and shamed, so be it. He loved the roads, he loved the food, its variety, and he loved the way it was eaten. He loved the pace of life, the empty spaces, the depth of culture and the Gallic shrug—he just loved France big time. So now, he was off once more to drink in its bounteous pleasures, a few weeks of indulgence out of a year of dreadful routine, general boredom, stress, strain, crap, and Christmas!

Denis the romantic never failed to experience a thrill whenever his feet, or on this occasion, the wheels of his car, touched French soil. Approaching his mid-century he found more and more solace in communicating with the great outdoors and if it happened to be outdoor France, even better.

Fairly squat, though not significantly overweight, Denis was conscious that without much effort he could be and so attempted to subscribe to a regime of healthy natural foods and healthy living. This attitude either sustained his love of the great outdoors, including cooking on an open barbecue and camping out under a starry sky or was sustained by it. Whichever the case, Denis was, generally, the kind of person who did not expect a lot out of life, but just a little now and then. His romanticism, however, could sometimes be out of concert with the practicalities and realities of life and he needed the ever-dependable Maisie to provide the necessary back-up.

Much to his wife's frustration, Denis's understanding of DIY was "Do It Yourself, Maisie". Still, she had long since learnt to make allowances for this and generally 'allowed' Denis to do his own thing, only reining him in occasionally.

Packed out with people and survival gear, and dragging behind it a life-support system consisting of a huge tent on wheels complete with cooker, pots, pans, in fact everything including a kitchen sink, the car, making its way steadily through the various checkpoints, headed towards the gaping mouth of the Brittany Ferries' ship *Duc de Normandie*.

Stuffed in the rear, suitcases bulged with clothes, not only for every meteorological eventuality but also for any possible or impossible disaster that might result in France being cordoned off from the rest of the world for a lengthy period.

In short, the party that set off was an entirely self-sufficient microcosm of twenty-first-century suburban life and provided a fairly complete cross-section of that society. The seven persons, including Denis, ranged from Jolly Jack the dribbling four-year-old, known affectionately as 'little fellah', to Maurice, the elder statesman of the group, a dribbling eighty-year-old, known respectfully as 'Granddad'.

Maurice was 'acoustically challenged'. He was thus stricken to the extent that when the lights went out on the campsite he became the Helen Keller of the great outdoors and if the 'lights out' happened to coincide with one of Maurice's regular expeditions to the ablutions, the general alert of 'Maurice is out' was sounded, and a search party had to be mustered and sent out to bring him back.

This contingency plan had arisen out of a rather unfortunate incident whilst camping in a Bavarian forest the previous year. Having been caught short in the middle of the night, Maurice, on leaving the washrooms in almost total darkness, had turned right instead of left and wandered off into the primeval forest. Poor Maurice spent the rest of the night stumbling from tree to tree, forlornly asking them if he was on the right road back to his tent. The fact that they didn't seem to answer him was, he believed, because they were still angry that we had won two World Wars and one World Cup!

Gloria's dad, Maurice Carter, a veteran with over twenty years service in Her Majesty's Navy, including being torpedoed twice in the Second World War, had seen it all. So the shenanigans he witnessed whilst on camping trips with his daughter and her friends, he generally took in his stride. Anyway, he had his own interests and distractions. In reality, Maurice was more the elder statesman than the senile octogenarian, which it sometimes suited him to appear as. Inside the naturally aged shell of an eighty-year-old body was a very lively mind. Maurice, diminutive and lean with a military posture, the legacy of his career at sea, was at the moment, securely ensconced somewhere in the back of the people carrier next to the door with the childlock on. Perched on his head was his ever-present Panama hat.

Denis was driving with Eddie, ably supported by the latest edition of the Reader's Digest map of the world, navigating. Eddie Lancaster the navigator, married to Gloria, was originally from 'sarf Landan' and spoke mainly in cockney rhyming slang which wasn't an invaluable asset whilst navigating for Denis who having grown up above the Watford Gap, did not always understand his friend's turn of phrase. When Eddie confidently advised Denis to follow the 'frog and toad', Denis spent the next ten minutes looking out for two Frenchmen!

Tall and slim, Eddie looked as if he had been stretched a little too much, though, being married to Gloria, he felt that he had experienced the rack on more than one occasion, and had a slight forward lean. He had a very easy-going personality, a fascination for all things mechanical and much preferred the quiet life to arguing too much with his dear spouse. Like Denis, he too enjoyed the great outdoors, though his passion was fishing.

With the help of a posse of Brittany Ferries' attendants, Denis managed to steer the car into the correct black hole in the middle of the boat carefully avoiding those either side (which would have led into the harbour), and the adventure had begun in earnest.

Denis's often critical, but essentially loyal wife, Maisie, with little fellah bouncing on her knee, was crushed up against daughter Clare. Maisie's practical side was a perfect foil to her husband's romantic nature. Whereas Denis's love of France had provided the rationale for the trip, Maisie's attention to the practical details ensured its feasibility. Maisie's early forties', trim body, contained a mind much younger in years, and with the encouragement of her bosom buddy Gloria, she felt that she could still enjoy the interests of late youth. A rather large bag containing most of the latest Avon catalogue

4

enabled them both to keep this illusion of the 'glam gals' largely intact.

Gloria was the more 'up front' of the double act. Tall and once naturally blonde, she was also in her early forties but, unlike her friend, was completely unable to hide her feelings, often throwing herself into situations without fully thinking them through. This usually involved members of the opposite sex, and, though completely loyal to Eddie, her husband of twenty-something years, she found herself often drawn feebly into awkward predicaments. Maisie was far more subtle in her approach and, when it came to handsome young men, generally allowed Gloria to set the trail. She was, however, very quick to catch up if she felt that her friend was getting too much of the upper hand. The rivalry that this could engender created the only times when the two were in conflict. Generally, they appeared more like twins separated at birth.

Denis and Maisie's daughter Clare, who had just been voted the female Kevin of the year, made Jeremiah seem like the Bible's funny guy. Riddled with hormones, her glass always seemed half-empty and, though she was looking forward to the holiday and would enjoy the next few weeks, it would be in a perversely begrudging way. She did find solace in her little 'bro' Jack, whom she loved and hated passionately and in equal measure. Whilst her teenage mood swings had her adolescent body up and down, Jack provided a healthy distraction, even if sometimes it was with thoughts of murder!

It was 3.15 in the afternoon and the boat was due to leave at 4.00. Before alighting from the car, Gloria had just enough time to touch up the war paint and to ask Maisie's opinion.

"Oh it's lovely," she sighed. "What do you think of mine?"

As the people carrier finally edged to a halt three millimetres from the car in front, Denis switched off the engine. The doors opened and the whole gang spilled out onto the floor of the car deck.

"Yeh I've seen that film with Woody Allen in it," reflected Denis, as the garage-hand smiled proudly at the closeness with which he had managed to park their vehicle to the one in front.

"Bloody nutter..."

Actually getting from the car deck, in the bowels of the vessel, to the more salubrious surroundings of the upper decks proved to be a tad trickier than negotiating the loading ramp had been. Flinging open car doors and dragging things through the tiny gaps left when as many vehicles as possible are crammed into a limited space, meant that by the time the party reached the stairs, the scratch count was impressive. It included two newish-looking people carriers, a bright red BMW and, best of all, an eighteen-inch beautifully clean-looking horizontal cut carved out by the buckle on Little Fellah's shoe, right down the side of a deep blue Mazda.

Even before reaching the passenger decks, Clare was already convinced that the on-board film would be boring, and Jack needed the toilet, as did Granddad. On the way to the exit of the car deck Eddie was waylaid after spotting a fascinating-looking contraption strapped to the back of glistening Saab or was it a Skoda? Whilst trying to squeeze between an old Morris 1100 and a caravan, to get a closer look, he had managed to snag the crotch of his trousers on the bonnet badge. By the time he had extricated himself, everyone else had disappeared up the steep steps and into the ship. The last sight Denis had was of Eddie apparently Sumo wrestling with the front end of a car!

"Stress," he thought. "Boy, does he need a holiday!"

A two-berth cabin was quickly organised, the bags dumped and they all made off to the bar to re-group and refuel; it didn't take Eddie long to find them, he knew where Denis would be.

Quite a few drinks later, the boat was well into the channel and the drinks were well into Eddie and Denis. Granddad was enjoying his G and Ts, Clare who had been carping to go to the film had been persuaded to take Little Fellah to see the magic show instead. Gloria and Maisie, well, having discovered that the white wine in an 'on-the-boat' white wine and lemonade consisted of a 33cl bottle, were more than contented, if a little noisy. Gloria's facial paint needed a little touching up but after three bottles of white wine, who cared?

Eddie, never a good traveller, was beginning to become aware of the boat's movement as the four pints of Stella had begun to oscillate from one side of his stomach to the other. As it seemed increasingly determined to escape back up his gullet, he decided to go for a lie-down, as did Granddad. Maisie, by now semi-conscious, wanted to see the film or at least sleep in the dark cinema. Denis reckoned that sharing a cinema with the girls was a better option than sharing a bed with Eddie or Maurice, and followed Gloria and Maisie in the direction of the cinema. After purchasing their tickets, they entered the small room where the film was being screened.

It wasn't until her eyes eventually had become accustomed to the darkness that Gloria realised there were really quite a number of people at the back of a seemingly empty room, and it was only the sound of their appreciative giggling at her theatrical entrance that had alerted her. Sheepishly, she settled down for the 'official' entertainment. Maisie and Denis had also enjoyed Gloria's warm-up routine; in fact, despite the film being heralded as 'film of the year', Gloria's performance was probably the only bit the whole audience had enjoyed all afternoon.

Clare, who had been desperate to see the other film, was stuck with Jack in the children's playroom. He was surrounded by similarly screaming kids being egged on by a magician, who recognising a responsive audience when he saw one, was milking every ear-piercing scream. Jack, purple-faced with disbelief at the magician's inability to spot it, was shrieking at the top of his stack, "It's there behind you!!!!"

Any notion of him passively agreeing to being removed from the bedlam really was a non-starter, so poor Clare's misery was complete.

"I knew it, I just knew it," she muttered.

When later they met up in the bar, they were all, apart from Jack, suffering from post-lubrication blues. He was still trying to get his head around the magician's apparent stupidity while Clare was wallowing in her grief and suffering from the mother of all migraines. Still it was time for food and that cheered everyone up.

It was a real feast, fresh crusty bread, thick creamy butter, slices of juicy ham, dripping mayonnaise all washed down with lashings of ginger beer. Unfortunately, on seeing the food, Eddie's stomach decided that enough was enough.

"Excuse me," he spluttered, rushing out as the Stella

finally found its way up to the exit. The sickly Eddie completed the journey to France back in his bunk, with Jack and Denis occupying the one above.

When the "Bonjour Mesdames et Messieurs...nous allons arriver a Roscoff bientôt..." was announced on the public address system, Eddie, by now feeling much better, was explaining to Jack the fascinating way in which the bunk bed could be turned into a seat and Gloria and Maisie were competing for pole position in front of the mirror. Granddad, who had not been seen since he went off to the toilet some time earlier that afternoon, was hopefully still somewhere on board. Denis was still asleep and Clare had gone off to the duty-free shop to buy some Belgium chocolate but they were just closing when she got there and wouldn't let her in.

"I knew it," she said, "I just knew it."

Keen to be straight off so as to get to the overnight campsite to take advantage of as much remaining daylight as possible, the gang re-grouped hurriedly. Just as they exited, they grabbed Granddad, who, with good fortune, happened to be passing the cabin door after completing his ninth circuit of the boat, and made straight for the car deck. While the announcement for car passengers to return to their vehicles was still trailing away, the excited party were once more crammed into the overloaded people carrier with Denis already revving the impatient engine waiting for the off. There was a tangible frisson—the air they were breathing was continental, they were a matter of minutes from France. Any moment now those huge bow doors would open and they would be speeding towards Perhidy in Brittany and their first night on French soil— they could hardly contain their excitement.

Forty minutes later the camera panned back to reveal that the once-crowded car deck was now completely empty, except that is, for just two vehicles, one a steamed-up, grey-coloured, people carrier, replete with seven rather disgruntled occupants; the other, which was what the steamed-up, grey coloured people carrier was waiting impatiently behind—a broken-down car and huge caravan.

By the time the front wheels of the car finally rolled onto French tarmac it was a completely dark moonless night.

"Bloody great!" thought Denis. "France in the dark!"

Eddie the navigator was equipped with the directions to the campsite, which had been thoughtfully sent in 'pidgin' English by the campsite proprietor.

Eddie was carefully trying to interpret the instructions by torchlight. They were like the instructions that you get with toys bearing the legend 'Made in China'.

'To find your way to Perhidy will be completely at ease.'

"Yeah, I'll bet," thought Eddie.

'When you pass over the railway tracks you will be right and straight and all that will be left is to go straight, right.

Before seeing in your left, a fork in the route, you will be right to take the left turn then you will be here.

Have a warm welcome. We hope your stay will be stimulating. Please, make less noise when you arrive in the night.'

Several slight detours later, the by now exhausted party arrived at Campsite Perhidy. It was gone eleven and the place was deathly silent until Jack, having been asleep for a good couple of hours, broke the silence with an excited shriek and the business of erecting tents began.

For Eddie and Gloria this was the first time that they had used their tent and this soon became apparent. The fact that their first attempt at its erection was in complete darkness did not make things any easier. However, Eddie, a master at all things that have to be put together, was gallantly trying to involve his dear wife in the maiden construction of their canvas boudoir. He was hoping that the romantic atmosphere, naturally created by first-night camping on a balmy July evening in the French countryside, might continue later on (ooh la la!).

Unfortunately, it seemed to Eddie that Gloria was wilfully trying her best to undermine any such thoughts. Despite all best efforts, Eddie, who had managed uncannily, to keep a lid on the steaming volcano which his patience had become, finally cracked. Having coped, through gritted teeth, with the constant moaning about what all this was doing to her nails, Gloria's final act of unconscious subversion was when she decided to take a little break. Leaning on the loosely draped canvas , which covered the spaghetti junction of poles and ropes out of which Eddie had carefully constructed the frame, she unceremoniously disappeared taking the whole lot with her.

Not tonight, Josephine!

As the dust settled, it didn't help Eddie when, whilst dragging Gloria out by her feet, he glanced over to see Maisie just putting the finishing touches to 'chez-nous'. Maisie who had been camping with Denis enough times to realise it was best to let him watch, soon had their temporary home in place and pegged down for the night. Denis, apart from having problems in constructing anything as complex as a deck chair, also had a 'dodgy'

back which meant that it helped him to dodge most forms of unpleasant physical activity. The gentle rubbing of that part of his anatomy was always a sign that Denis was ready for some serious spectating. He did, at one point, consider offering some brotherly advice to Eddie but thought better of it, just before Gloria hit the canvas, as it were. Eddie's frustration was complete when the campsite manager made an appearance to ask the party to 'please be whispering' as everyone was sleeping. To our intrepid travellers, being told off for making a noise was as much part of the holiday as insect bites and sunburn, so, already developing his own Gallic shrug, Denis, in his best French, said, "Pardon," and Monsieur le Patron went off relatively happy.

Eventually everything was set up ready for occupation; all that was left now was the trip to the ablutions and that should be a piece of gateau. This was when they realised that Granddad had already taken himself off in search of the toilets; how long he had been gone goodness only knew.

It was Denis who found Maurice struggling with the lighting system at the sinks. The lights were on timers, which sadly didn't quite last long enough for Maurice to get from the switch to the sink before it cut out. Time after time Maurice took on the challenge, time after time the switch just beat him. Denis, arriving like the cavalry, put his hand up reassuringly to Granddad and with a smug smile, pressed his hand firmly on the switch while Granddad shuffled over to the sink with triumph on his face.

"Gotcha!" crowed Denis, just as all the lights went out.

"Oh for goodness sake, I don't believe this!" Exasperation echoed in his voice.

The whole campsite was in complete darkness.

"Stand still, don't move, Granddad," pleaded Eddie.

"Granddad!" But Granddad had already set off back to the tent. "Granddad's out! Granddad's out!" the cry went up.

By the time the worried party trudged back to the tents, half an hour later, Maisie was waiting to greet them.

"What's up, where have you lot been?"

"It's Maurice," panted Denis. "We've lost him."

"So who's that snoring in his tent then?" said Maisie. "He's been in bed for ages."

As Denis lay contented in his bed looking out of the net window into the starry sky and drinking in the cool night air he leaned over and said,

"You can't beat it, can you, Maisie?"

Maisie grunted. "Get on your own side, Denis."

"No," repeated Denis, "you can't beat camping."

Chapter Two

Up bright and early, washed, fed and ready for the road, just as dawn's bright sunshine was warming away the cool morning dew, was not quite how things worked out the next day. The previous night's excitement, the long voyage across the briny and of course the liquid refreshment had all taken their toll on any perfect dreams of an early start.

Eddie struggled out of bed first, accidentally dragging Gloria with him after becoming snagged in the covers of the compact and bijoux camp bed. This woke up Maurice who immediately needed the toilet. In his hurry he fell out of bed, knocking over the pans which Gloria had told Eddie to put away into the camp kitchen the night before. When Denis's head poked through the previously zipped-up entrance, the three of them were rolling on the floor, a mixture of blankets, pans and bodies,

"I see you're up then," he noted observantly.

The general mayhem in next door's tent had woken up Clare who couldn't believe that she'd been disturbed so early. Jack who some time during the night had spanned the great divide between the two beds was snuggled up next to his mum. Maisie, being capable of sleeping through most things, was oblivious to the fact that morning was upon them.

After finishing his morning cuppa, and rather a sweaty ham bap from the previous day's packed lunch, Denis, his warm feet shoved into a pair of cold damp trainers, shuffled off to find the loos for his morning constitutional. On the way he met Granddad who was on his way back from another successful expedition to the ablutions,

"Morning, Maurice," he said as he went past.

Maurice, concentrating hard to find his way back to the tent, didn't see him or hear him.

Denis smiled to himself: "Good old Maurice," he thought. "Deaf bugger."

The morning's daylight illuminated the Spartan nature of the 'free', first night campsite and by the time he had reached the toilets Denis was under no illusion as to what he would find. French toilets were, after all said and done, as much a part of the French character as baguettes and stripy jumpers, and, anyway, he had to 'go'.

Having carefully inspected the line of cabinets, searching for the least grim one, he was faced with a dilemma: should he go for the slightly cleaner one or the one with the lock that worked? Realising he needed to decide quickly, he plumped for the relative cleanliness of the end closet. This meant straddling the hole in the ground with his head pressed firmly against the door whilst both hands were pushing against the wall, desperately trying to stop himself from sliding down onto the floor. Concentrating hard on sustaining this precarious position, Denis cut a delightful figure. He was well aware that any false move and the meticulously lined-up cruise missile might well end up scudding into the boxer shorts, stretched invitingly between his ankles. Having successfully negotiated all of the potential hazards, and, mission accomplished, the smile of satisfaction melted off Denis's face with the realisation that, unlike English toilets, French ones don't provide paper. He hadn't quite finished thinking, "I don't believe this," when a very determined fellow camper shoved hard on the door and Denis, momentarily distracted, was caught offguard. His feet slipped backwards, whilst his fingernails scraped painfully down the walls. As his forehead hit the concrete floor, a face appeared around the door:

"Oh pardon, monsieur, pardon."

Back at base, Gloria and Maisie, having just finished the day's first makeover, were comparing nails. Eddie was halfway through his third bowl of cereal, Jack, having discovered how the pegs came out of the ground, was helping to take the tent down, and Clare was still in bed. Nobody was sure where Maurice was. The girls looked up just as Denis appeared around the hedge onto the site

" Ooh—do you know you've got a big red bump on your forehead, Denis love?"

"Don't," said Denis, through gritted teeth. "Just don't."

It took rather longer than anticipated to strike camp. If Eddie couldn't believe how useless Gloria was at erecting the tent in the dark, then he hadn't witnessed her helping to take it down in broad daylight. After two hours of contributing very little to the objective, Eddie had, once again, lost his patience with his darling wife and she joined Denis as a spectator. To be fair to her, she had been a little bit distracted from the task, worrying about Granddad who had not been seen since shortly after breakfast.

Denis, still licking his wounds from his earlier trauma, was hugely cheered up watching Eddie and Gloria. Eddie, having finally managed to get the huge canvas down, was exasperated by an annoying lump that wouldn't flatten out. Determined to pack it down neatly, he disappeared under the sheet to confront the offending bulge, a few minutes later a muffled voice came from under the covers:

"I've found Granddad!"

Hence forward, the exhortation 'Check the tent' joined 'Granddad's out' in the list of useful phrases for camping with Maurice.

By midday, the happy campers were on their merry way. Even Clare had been hugely cheered by the morning's shenanigans, and the way in which Denis kept gingerly feeling the lump on his forehead reduced her to fits of quiet giggles in the back of the car as she tried to imagine the scene behind the toilet door.

The plan was to head for the little town of Morgat situated on the Crozon Peninsula where they would visit an old friend, Monique, whom Maisie had met whilst on a school French exchange trip years before.

Eddie had managed to locate their position on the map and off they went, heading south towards Le Faou and their planned lunch break.

The smoothness of the journey, broken only by the occasional swerve as Denis tried to catch a glimpse of his forehead in the mirror, meant that it wasn't long before the previous late night had caught up with everyone, and the contents of the back of the car had descended into slumbers.

"Bloody typical, eh, Eddie?" said Denis seeing Maisie's open gob snoring in the back. "Everybody sleeping."

But Eddie didn't reply.

They arrived at the Supermarché at Le Faou just in time for that quaint French custom the 'siesta', which meant that any hopes of buying provisions for lunch were dashed for at least two hours, so they set off for the centre of town to look for a café instead. On the way, when Denis missed a give-way sign, they experienced that other quaint French delicacy the 'indignant driver'. The bloke that Denis cut up seemed to use both hands and both legs to remonstrate with him. Denis in turn, smiled, gave a friendly wave and mouthed,

"Go boil your head, Jacques."

It wasn't long before the group were settled outside a cosy French café and they were all feeling somewhat better for a drink. Now to try out the French lingo on the unsuspecting waitress... . Eddie who had no inhibitions about trying out his French was always prepared to insert both the words he knew into any situation; besides, he had always subscribed to the theory that whatever his conversation lacked in content could always be made up for with volume.

"Bonjour," he bellowed. "Five coffees and two cokes, si'l vous plaît," the last part being delivered with a definite pause between each word, giving it the kind of conviction that seemed to say,

"So there you have it."

Denis, whose schoolboy French, had actually progressed through previous visits to France, had been carefully piecing together in his mind what he would say to her. He was quietly impressed with Eddie's success using the 'cut out the middle man' method of communicating in a foreign language but knew that his more refined skills would be required to order some tucker.

Unfortunately, as is the norm in these cases, as soon as Denis gave an indication that he knew a couple of words of the host language the person he was speaking to immediately assumed that he was fluent and launched into a veritable stream of colloquial French. His companions sat listening with admiration especially when Denis punctuated the stream with an occasional 'oui' and 'non'.

When the conversation concluded, Denis wasn't quite sure whether the cook was 'knackered', the cooker was 'knacked', or the kitchen was completely dysfunctional. But what he did know was that the food was off and that they wouldn't be getting any nourishment at that particular bistro.

"Well?" they all asked with baited breath. "What's for lunch?"

He broke the news to the starving crew as gently as possible and when they asked why, he thought it best to cover all bases, muttering something about it was too late for food and, anyway, the chef was dead and the kitchen had been taken out by an exploding chip pan.

"I don't believe this," chimed in Clare, whose usual low misery threshold suddenly dropped several more points on the Richter scale of pessimism.

And so it was off to Morgat, calling at a large *supermarché* on the way which, by the time they got there, would be open again and they would soon all be fed and happy. After all the drinks they had consumed while Denis had been negotiating his way around his first French conversation for several years, they all had to 'make water' before setting off. The toilets in the square across from the café were very convenient except that halfway through a very satisfying stream Denis realised that he was on complete view to the rest of the population of Le Fiou. Fortunately, the only ones sad enough to feel it was amusing were Maisie, Gloria and Clare whose juvenile girly giggles alerted him to his exposed position.

"Ah yes," thought Denis as he was reminded of another of those little endearing French idiosyncrasies—very 'public' toilets—which contributed to making France the attraction it was.

It didn't take that long to reach Morgat, but, despite this, Denis was soon once again accompanied by a bunch of Rip Van Winkles, apart that was from Eddie, who had come into his own as navigator. He was enjoying tracking the progress of the windy road as it snaked its way along the course of the River Aulne, on its way towards the Atlantic coast.

"Cor blimey," uttered Eddie, wide-eyed with admiration when halfway there he spotted the huge suspension bridge spanning the river. Any form of construction or contraption and Eddie was happy. Whilst he drooled over the complex structure of the bridge, Denis was trying to concentrate on negotiating the steep and twisting banks of the river, at the same time himself admiring the magnificent scenery that the bridge spanned.

"Wow!" he said.

The passengers in the back were singularly unimpressed as they snoozed on.

"Philistines!" grumbled Eddie.

"Morons!" thought Denis.

Arriving eventually at Crozon, Denis bathing in the euphoria of having successfully negotiated a route following traffic signs in a foreign language, absentmindedly drove on past the main shopping thoroughfare and onto Morgat which was singularly bereft of any Le Clercs, Intermarchés or even Super 'U's. Always the practical one, Maisie now awake and ready once again to take over the reins of Denis's life, enquired as to what they were meant to do for lunch. It kind of put a damper on his growing, if still very much embryonic sense of adequacy, which had sprung from his confident handling of the driving. With icy sarcasm she continued,

"It's just that Clare's having a major stress, Jack's just eaten a fly and Granddad died five minutes ago; apart from that I'm sure we could all survive for a few more days."

Gloria, ever the peacemaker, suggested that after they had arrived at Monique's, whilst Maisie and Eddie got sorted out with the tents, she and Denis could do the shopping for provisions. Denis quite warmed to this idea, as although he genuinely loved the middle section of camping, he never did like the bits at either end. He was also beginning to feel his dodgy back coming on when the thought occurred to him of Maisie perhaps setting up camp first and then going shopping as well, an even more attractive idea! But he thought better of suggesting it.

When they arrived at the sleepy little group of cottages, one of which was Monique's, a rather anxious-looking neighbour pointed them in the right direction. As she caught a glimpse into the back of the car she did her Gallic shrug and muttered something which they didn't quite catch, but it wasn't 'Bien venue'.

Monique bounced out from the front of the cottage, genuinely pleased to see them. After the customary exchange of kisses, several on each cheek, she explained how to get to the back of the cottage and the field that would be their campsite for the next few days. After negotiating some country lanes and several fields, they all arrived at the rear of the domicile and parked up. Monique continued with the welcome routine ending with the question,

"Have you eaten?"

Before Gloria could finish saying, "Well, me and Denis were going to..." Maisie said, "No!"

"That is great..." continued Monique; they had all been waiting for the 'Engleeesh' to arrive before they ate and there they all were, gathered on the patio under the window awaiting them, all being Monique's son, Christian, Brother Albert, his wife Bernice, with girls, Giselle and Fabienne and son Armand, Monique's sister Lisette and friends, Pierre and Collette and children Marco, Jean-Claud and Patrice.

Like our intrepid travellers, they too had been holding out to eat but, despite their gaunt and lean faces which were covetously eyeing the spread of food, the rituals had first to be observed and so it was, "Bonjour, bonjour," kiss-kiss, kiss-kiss,

"Ca va?"

"Oui, oui. Ca va."

"Bonjour." Kiss, kiss, kiss.

"Bonjour."

"Oui oui."

"Bonjour." Kiss, kiss, kiss.

"Bonjour, bonjour, bonjour." Kiss-kiss-kiss.

"Oui, oui, oui, ça va, bonjour, bonjour, bonjour...
................and finally...the food.

"Come to the table," came the invitation and the hungry travellers needed no second prompting. Monique had prepared a lovely spread of sliced cold meats, paté, cheeses, tasty local tomatoes in a home-made dressing. Lots of fresh bread, melon and of course plenty of wine. Some time later, reinvigorated with good food and fine wine, it was time to put up the tents. Monique led them to a strip of land, which belonged to the cottage, but, when they arrived, the local members of the land preservation society were all out in full force protecting their individual square hectares. Like other cute French customs such as peeing in public and playing chicken on country roads, when it comes to 'no trespassing' on my bit of terra firma, the French really did take the twice cooked. To add to the endearing cuteness, the parcel of land which makes up the back of small French country properties is sliced up in precise pieces with no apparent regard for the fact that a piece of land two feet wide by twenty feet long is neither use nor ornament. Still with a bit of horse trading, Monique managed to acquire enough land to be able to pitch the tents. Unfamiliar with the sight of state-of-the-art camping gear, their French friends looked on in amazement whilst Eddie and Maisie set about transforming a very plain-looking box on wheels into an eight-berth house. Monique et al stood for a while Gallic shrugging before they all wandered off, leaving them to it.

Gloria and Denis, bored at the thought of setting up

camp, had headed off to the nearest *hypermarché* to buy provisions for the next day. Clare couldn't decide whether a shopping trip with two adults was preferable to watching the tent unfold and before she had made up her mind, the shoppers had left so she was left with her usual chore of entertaining Jack. Granddad went for a wander.

The trouble with shopping in a *hypermarché* is the amount and variety of the goods on display. It is well known that when it comes to food the French philosophy is: 'If it moves it's edible, if it doesn't it's probably still worth a try anyway.' One result of this open-minded approach to gastronomy is that, when standing in a *hypermarché* at one end of the fish food counter, it is remarkably difficult to see the far end. This being because every available shell-inhabiting creature, that lives either in the sea or on the shoreline, is available in your average French supermarket, most still alive, and many still moving, in a state of shock and wondering why the tide hasn't come in.

Trying to complete your grocery shopping in a *hypermarché* amidst the distractions of the full range of French meats, fish, cheeses, fruit, vegetables, et cetera would be quite a challenge for your steely focussed, SAS trained weekly shopper: for Gloria it was quite impossible.

Gloria shopped like other people breathed; it was not something she could cope with thinking about or even make a decision on, she just did it. To Gloria a one-Euro piece meant only one thing, a shopping trolley. If Gloria could have controlled two trolleys at once she would have done; as it was she struggled with one, but what she lacked in the skills to manoeuvre the trolley she more than compensated for with her ability to fill it.

With her mouth dry, her knees shaking and her palms clammy, she could not wait to get into the main body of the store and begin. In her eagerness to get 'stuck in', she began by smacking into the automatic doors, wrongly assuming that their speed of opening would be proportionate to her level of enthusiasm. Having recovered her composure, she headed straight for the....well, she just headed straight for anything—at least, as straight as your average shopping trolley allows.

It is a commonly held misconception that shopping trolleys for some mysterious reason develop mechanical faults shortly after commission and that for similarly mysterious reasons nobody is able to correct them. In reality, they are cleverly designed by the manufacturers to wander purposely all over the shop so that the hardiest and most single-minded shopper is exposed within temptation distance to just about everything on offer. Putting wobbly wheels on Gloria's shopping trolley was like putting a sign on a children's playground saying, 'Please stick your head through the railings.' It was completely unnecessary; it simply meant that she visited things in a different order. The end product was always the same, a massively overburdened trolley, impossible to move.

In contrast to Gloria's 'modus operandi', which could be neatly summed up as, 'if it's on the shelf it should be in the trolley', Denis was a 'hunter gatherer'. Prowling the aisles in search of good deals, he shopped alone, his ears and eyes alert to any potential bargains. Wherever he saw two or three fellow shoppers gathering, he was there checking out trolleys, scanning adjacent shelves to see if he'd missed anything. His greatest triumph had been one time when he had bought a reduced price, 'buy one get one free', close-to-sell-by-date, pack of pork chipolatas, which, with their 'special offer' status, meant that by the time he had reached the checkout, he was actually owed money! What he did miss in France was the absence of yellow stickers denoting, for one reason or another, a reduced price. Paradoxically, it seemed that though the French were prepared to eat anything, they were very fussy about what they ate. It is a case of 'that is the price—take it or leave it'.

This didn't however diminish Denis's fascination for the enormous variety of foodstuffs on offer and he was perfectly content strolling around the Epicurean heaven of a giant Le Clerc, marvelling at the fascinating variety of the goods available and breathing in the very gastronomic culture which contributed to him being such a Francophile. Having said that, he particularly liked to visit the booze department.

The 'booze crooze', having become something of a pilgrimage, had originated for people on the south coast of England and steadily spread northwards. It had been one of the first flirtations, which had led to Denis's love affair with France. Cases of beer, cartons of red wine and half-price whisky, never mind the fags, had more than justified the cost of a 'nipping across' the channel at special winter rates.

Travelling out on a Friday night and returning on the Saturday, various combinations of Denis and Maisie, Denis, Eddie and Gloria, Denis and his mates had for several years been 'booze running' from the North Breton coast of Roscoff, rattling and rolling out of the bowels of the

Duc de Normandie and breathing a sigh of relief when ushered through 'Her Majesty's Customs and Excise'. It wasn't that the excess baggage had been part of any huge smuggling network but mainly a few too many fizzy wines or the extra bottle of spirits. But having once witnessed the contents of one family's holiday vehicle spread across the tarmac of the dock side on the wrong side of the security fence like some giant Damien Hirst sculpture, they had always approached the exit gates with trepidation. Consequently, every successful and unmolested passage through the magic gates of customs was greeted with hysterical and excessive whelps of delight accompanied with ironic shouts of 'Gotcha this time, you bastards!'—followed by a chorus of "ere we go, 'ere we go, 'ere we go'.

Since the recent relaxation of the restrictions on the amount which could be legally brought in, a lot of the fun had gone out of 'booze running'. A lot, but certainly not all of it!

Denis stood contemplating the rows of bottles, converting Euros into pounds and sighing at the thought of the deals on offer. But this was not 'booze shopping', this was 'provisions for tonight's meal shopping'. So, reluctantly, he pulled himself away from the potential booty to concentrate on the evening meal.

Gloria, on the other hand, had long since collapsed in exhaustion at one of an endless row of checkouts having managed to guide her recalcitrant 'chariot' back to base full of purchases that had nothing to do with that night. When Denis caught up with her, she was in a discussion with the girl on the till about tomatoes.

"Yes, I have tomatoes. Yes these are tomatoes, to-ma-toes," insisted Gloria.

Unfortunately Gloria had forgotten to weigh the tomatoes before coming to the checkout. The young girl, in contrast to Gloria, remained remarkably calm but was having problems communicating this oversight to her. Gloria who recognising the word tomatoes was feeling quite smug that she was actually having a conversation in French, albeit consisting of just one word, that being 'tomatoes'. By the time Denis arrived, the girl on the checkout was surrounded by a supportive group of shrugging and very indignant locals who were trying to explain to an oblivious Gloria that she was supposed to have weighed the chuffing tomatoes before she came to the chuffing checkout.

"Yes, TOMATOES," repeated an increasingly agitated Gloria, still waiting for the centime to drop.

Denis, who was naturally calm in moments of crisis, and being further buoyed up by the fact that he was obviously the closest thing to the cavalry, immediately recognised the problem and quietly ushered Gloria to the vegetable stall and rectified the error.

The group of indignant locals slowly dispersed comforted from having had their long-held prejudices about anyone foreign, particularly the English, confirmed by the fact that this strange English woman did not know about the need to have her tomatoes weighed—my God, whatever next!

And so eventually off to the car meandered Gloria and Denis, complete with tonight's tea in one trolley and half of the Le Clerc in the other, Denis satisfied after another successful hunting expedition, and Gloria...well just satisfied: she had spent a good hour in a big shop with an empty trolley.

"If heaven isn't any better than this," thought Gloria, "I ain't going!"

By the time shoppers got back to base camp the engineers had finished the construction of the tents and preparations soon got underway to transform the shopping into the evening meal. *Julien*, a nice white chewy fish, the English equivalent of which Denis was not quite sure, for the adults, *boeuf hachées* for the kids, *ratatouille* 'à la Maisie', consisting of tomatoes, courgettes, aubergine, shallots, garlic and her secret ingredient, which for obvious reasons nobody knew. This was accompanied by boiled, un-peeled new potatoes and crisp French green beans. The whole thing was washed down with plenty of liquid. Denis was never very good at deciding which drink was best to accompany the evening barbecue so by way of compromise he'd brought beer as an aperitif, wine as an accompaniment and local cider as a digestive. These were not necessarily consumed in the correct order but by the time that they had been topped off with a couple of generous shots of duty-free whisky, purchased during the ferry crossing, the end result was usually the same.

By the end of the evening, the gang of four were all in agreement that another good time had been had by all. Denis and Eddie were 'besht' pals and they all retired to their camp beds to spend a peaceful night punctuated only by the sounds of zips and splashing water as in turn each of the adults finally gave in to the nagging discomfort of a groaning bladder.

Chapter Three

The next day the revellers awoke to the awful sound of precipitation on canvas, rain! Rain was what every camper, even the most seasoned, Denis included, hoped at all costs to avoid during any tenting holiday. The sound of falling rain came second only to the sound of breaking wind on the campers' list of dreadful sounds, the latter being potentially the more lethal but tending to be the more transient. For some mysterious reason, as far as Denis could see, when rain descended on a campsite, it never seemed to take on the role of a passing shower but more often than not locked on like some heat-seeking missile determined to wreak havoc.

As anyone who had ever experienced the pleasures of life in the outdoors knew, there was no middle ground to camping, it was either heaven or hell. Apart from plagues of hungry mosquitoes or finding oneself on an overcrowded campsite resembling a Mexico City ghetto, or pitching next to the neighbours from hell, nothing was more effective than rain for changing the nature of the great outdoors. It was capable of transforming Camelot into Hades, relaxed, easygoing comrades into short-tempered antagonists and idyllic countryside ambrosias into slimy mud-ridden battlefields.

Rain, however lightly falling on a tent, always has the ability to sound like it is coming down like stair rods. The result of this is that any sleep experienced during falling rain tends to be of the fitful variety. Consequently, much of the irritability brought on by a damp tent, damp clothes, and the odd drip, usually in the face, owes its origins to previous events. Unfortunately on this particular morning, the rain was indeed coming down in stair rods and, to make matters worse, when the party had hit the sack the night before, it was at the end of a seemingly balmy July evening. Denis, the romantic, wishing to feel the breeze on his face had not, contrary to the advice of Maisie, the practical one, zipped down the window in the side of the tent. Now, with the assistance of a prevailing wind, Denis was lying in a veritable pool of rainwater, which had been unceremoniously dumped on his sleeping bag.

"Great," thought Denis.

Neither was his mood helped by the fact that curled up next to him, as 'snug as a bug' in the proverbial 'rug', and totally oblivious to her husband's plight, was the aforementioned Maisie, for whom Denis had spent the night acting as a particularly efficient windbreak.

Denis suspected that it may well have just been his paranoia but etched across her slumbering face seemed to be the words, "I told you so, Denis."

"Great, bloody great," thought Denis.

He was almost beginning to enjoy perversely the hopelessness of his plight when the sounds from the tent opposite cheered him up.

Just like Denis, Eddie had discovered that the rains had arrived long before his comatose partner had begun to stir. But, unlike Denis, he hadn't yet discovered that it had invaded his boudoir, at least not until he swung his legs around and plopped his feet into the little stream which was making its merry way through the middle of the tent. It was then that Denis heard the first of the "Oh Gawds!".

Eddie's tent, although effectively impervious to the driving wind and rain, had been inadvertently pitched astride an ancient watercourse, which only appeared during flash floods, one of which was at that very moment taking place. Peering outside, Eddie was just in time to see in the distance one of his socks bobbing up and down in a rivulet of water, heading rapidly towards another tributary before disappearing into a further torrent heading down from an adjacent field. Experiencing the kind of paranoia which would have impressed Denis, Eddie was convinced that his sock had waved at him just before disappearing around a little hummock at the end of the field.

"Oh Gawd!" cried Eddie.

At this point Eddie's attention was distracted by the sight of Maurice who, at some time during the night, had manoeuvred himself so that his head was sticking out of the tent canvas, exposing himself to the elements. He was lying there open-mouthed, facing upwards and apparently enjoying a very refreshing dream involving desert islands and jacuzzis, whilst the rain beat down on his toothless face.

"Oh my Gawd!" repeated Eddie, this time with even more feeling.

By this time the noise and general excitement had roused Maisie and also Gloria who on spying Granddad had woken everybody else up with a series of high-pitched screams interspersed with cries of,

"Oh Eddie, is he dead? Has he drowned?"

Eddie was at that moment more occupied with attempting to grab his other sock which seemed determined to join its partner down river and was not too bothered whether Maurice was alive or dead. Distracted by the screaming and leaning too far forward, he fell headlong into the rapidly expanding stream. The subsequent howls of shock from Eddie and screams from Gloria had plucked Maurice unceremoniously from the tranquillity of his desert island. Sitting up too quickly he too lost his balance, rolled off the bed, and fell on top of Eddie, both of them sliding out into the open air.

Denis who had long since forgotten his own plight had been listening intently to the drama unfolding opposite and unable to contain himself any longer chose this moment to see what was going on.

"Oh Gawd!" he said, as he stuck his head out of the tent flap. "You won't believe this, Maisie."

By the time Eddie and Granddad had been extricated from the water and Maurice had completed his course of counselling for post-traumatic stress disorder, it was rapidly approaching lunchtime.

In this respect, the dramatic events of the morning had been a blessing in disguise. The more usual pattern of camping dictated by wet weather is, wake up much earlier than usual because of the noise of the rain, too cold and wet to lounge around. Nobody can be arsed to traipse all the way to the sinks in the pouring rain to wash the previous night's unwashed dishes so breakfast is 'continental'. This means that as early as ten o'clock everybody has finished their soggy cereals and damp jam baguettes and are already saying, 'Right, what's happening today then?'

To be fair, jolly Jack was too young to recognise that when it came to camping there were such things as good days and bad days. As far as he was concerned the whole experience was one long adventure and, much to his sister's annoyance, he had been happily making dens out of the duvet he shared with Clare. Clare in turn had long since given up any hope of staying in bed with 'that idiot'.

To prevent her stress levels from hitting the canvas ceiling she had taken an early opportunity to retreat to the car to keep warm. Clutching a copy of *Chat* magazine and muttering about hating camping and she always had done, et cetera, et cetera, she had fallen asleep again on the back seat, unfortunately, missing most of the fun.

The answer to what to do when it starts to rain whilst camping was what all campers do in wet weather—they visit the nearest town. So, a while later, crammed into the Espace with the windows completely steamed up, they headed off to the picturesque Breton town of Quimper, capital of the Finistere region.

Shopping was going through the minds of the gals, culture was drying up Denis's damp thoughts. Eddie was going to investigate the French approach to fishing by visiting a few angling emporia. Maurice was attracted by the chance to visit the famous Quimper pottery works whose famous blue and yellow designs were featured on an old tin of biscuits he had once won in a church raffle many years ago (which he now kept his 'odd bits' in). Clare couldn't think of any reason why anyone would want to wander round an old historic town in the rain and also knew that she would end up looking after Jack so her happiness was complete.

"It stands on the confluence of the Odet and Steir rivers," offered Denis nonchalantly.

"Quimper," he continued a bit louder, rather optimistically believing they hadn't heard him.

"And it's got a Gothic Cathedral."

On hearing the last two words, Clare sat bolt upright. The word cathedral immediately hit Clare full force. "Oh no!" she thought, realising at once the significance of this seemingly innocent observation. Having frequently suffered from her dad's preoccupation with French churches, she knew straightaway that he had just announced an ABC tour—'Another Bloody Cathedral!' The implications of Denis's remark had not been lost on Maisie either, another long-suffering victim of Denis's obsession, but she had no intention of suffering today, she had her contingency plan all ready.

As they pulled into the car park in the town's square, Maisie prepared the way for her little bit of subterfuge:

"Er, just in case we get separated," she remarked casually, "this is where we'll meet at three o'clock. Okay?"

Having clearly established this particular contingency plan, they followed Denis off in the direction of their first objective.

Within ten minutes of them entering the magnificent Gothic building, they had managed to lose Denis. As Denis did not generally know his apse from his belfry, this had not taken too much effort.

Having unloaded Denis, the next stop was the famous Quimper pottery works. Maurice was pleased at the opportunity to visit the origins of his 'odd bits' tin and led the way with enthusiasm, if a little slowly. Somewhere along the way, they lost Eddie, or at least Eddie wandered off looking for his tackle shop, so the party that entered the factory shop had now been reduced to five.

It wasn't long before it became clear that small plates going at £30 a hit and small energetic boys, likely to provide the hit, was not a good mix. So, with the help of a substantial bribe, the result of some hard bargaining, Clare went off happily with Jack to explore Quimper, while Gloria and Maisie accompanied Maurice around the shop and into the pottery factory. Maisie and Gloria viewed the visit to the pottery factory as a minor detour before the main attraction, an afternoon of their favourite pastime, shopping.

Eddie managed to find his tackle shop and in his enthusiasm to explore the 'Aladdin's Cave' of fishermen's friends, he announced his entrance by tripping over the doorstop. Not being able to hold conversation of any length or meaning in a foreign language, he had hoped to sneak in and have the chance to take a good look at all the exciting gear on display before attracting the attention of the owner. His optimistic intention had been to identify some attractive-looking lures or other innovative equipment which would increase the chances of ending up with a fish on the end of a hook, choose the best one to purchase, and then simply finalise the deal. Unfortunately the loud noise and the even louder 'Oh Gawd' which accompanied the trip, dashed any chance of that and the little man who appeared, as if by magic, launched into a stream of conversation offering all the help that a potential purchaser may need.

"Ah bonjour," began Eddie confidently enough and that was it really. He then spent the next twenty minutes nodding approvingly when he felt it was appropriate and throwing in the odd authoritative 'Ah oui' as if in total concert with his newly discovered confrère, whilst in actual fact, he didn't have a clue what the little man was on about. The result was, that instead of leaving the shop with a couple of brightly coloured rubber worms, he fell out of the shop in a similar way to which he had fallen in, except this time struggling with a new polycarbonate rod and a huge state-of-the-art tripod to rest it on. He was reassured that his purchase had been a good one by the smiles of the shopkeeper as he helped Eddie out of the shop but wondered what the exultant "Oui!" meant just as the door closed.

All he had to do now was convince Gloria of the wisdom of spending a hundred and fifty quid on fishing gear— that might be tricky, he thought, with some understatement. So clattering off down the street, trying not to look too much like an impulse buyer, he made his way rather sheepishly to the car park.

Meanwhile Denis, who had finished his tour of the cathedral, began his search for the others. He spent at least fifteen minutes going round and round the church, rather sadly believing that they might still have been in there, before wandering out into the now brightening day. By this time, the heat of the mid-summer sun, which was increasingly appearing from behind the heavy dark clouds, was causing steam to rise from the rain-soaked pavements. Denis was beginning to get a little clammy dressed in his several layers of storm-proof clothing which, several hours ago, seemed appropriate. Now he was off searching for the others. Though he was keen to rejoin his fellow campers he was irresistibly attracted by the market and, wandering in, soon forgot about finding them.

Clare and Jack had also found the market but the one they were wandering around was the open-air one. Jack couldn't wait to spend the money which Clare had passed on to him and tried to buy just about anything that they happened to come across. It started with garden furniture, a huge oval table and six matching moulded plastic chairs, which to Jack had seemed a good idea, being just the sort of thing his mum would love in the garden. By the time Clare had stopped him from buying a fully-grown Capuchin monkey, he was getting pretty damned frustrated with his chaperone and began to get positively bolshie.

"I hate you!" he declared with passion. "You're a pig. A big one!" he added as an afterthought.

It was only the sight of live chickens that prevented Jack from mounting a full-scale coup. The chickens were being bid for by an excited crowd, mainly of elderly women, who were determined to prove that there is indeed no French word for 'queuing'. It wasn't, however, the sound of the noisy bartering which had caught Jack's attention nor the odd, less than elegant scuffles that kept breaking out over particularly plump-looking fowl. No, what Jack, and, for that matter, Clare found irresistible, was the way in which the Madame in charge of the proceedings was dispatching the purchased hens into cardboard boxes ready for removal by the satisfied buyers.

Picked up unceremoniously by the legs, they were flung upside down, wings a-flapping and shoved headfirst into fairly modest looking cardboard boxes. One hen, two hens, three hens—it didn't seem to matter, they were all thrust in, flaps down, adhesive tape applied and off they went with their new, satisfied owners.

Clare stood, open-mouthed, totally transfixed by the whole performance, before the sudden appearance of one particularly large chicken, rising skywards like some over-blown phoenix and landing neatly on the flag pole of the adjacent town hall brought her out of her trance. As the chicken stood balancing precariously on the horizontal pole, trying to summon up as much dignity as it could through its ruffled feathers, Clare realised that Jack had disappeared and simultaneously realised exactly where he was.

Being just big enough to be able to see the dispatching of the birds and small enough to be able to see the little coop in which they were housed, he had crawled under the market stall and neatly lifting the peg from the catch on the door, released into the wild the incarcerated chickens. At first they stumbled out looking rather bemused, blinking in the bright sunlight but they soon found their feet, or wings as it were, and off they shot. The ensuing mayhem was, even for Clare, who had experienced some choice moments witnessing adults erecting tents, something to behold.

"I don't believe it," she thought, just as the fun began.

Screaming stall-holders competed with indignant customers, all scrambling to grab the excited quarry and either return them to the enclosure or make off with them into the crowd. The kerfuffle attracted the attention of the local gendarmes who with whistles blowing, rather than encouraging any sort of calm, only added to the disorder.

It was as they came running in that the first stall was sent flying, adding even more to the chaos, bemused chickens became hysterical chickens and some of the curious onlookers opportunistic felons as a variety of merchandise went scuttling across the cobbled streets. This turned already enraged stall-holders into furious ones. Fights broke out and arrests were made as market day in Quimper turned into something resembling the opening scene from *Saving Private Ryan*. In the corner of the square stood Denis who had just emerged from the indoor market. He was shaking his head in disbelief and not a little admiration at the sight that was laid out before him.

"Bloody amazing," he thought. "Bloody amazing."

At the other side of the square Clare was trying her best to exit the scene before anyone who may have witnessed Jack appearing from under the table had connected his appearance with what had then unfolded.

"Put it down!" she screamed quietly at him, referring to the chicken whose wing he was clutching in his right hand.

"Down, NOW!"

"I hate you, you're a pig, a big fat one. I really hate you," he screamed back as she grabbed him by the jacket and without a backward glance dragged him up a little lane and off towards the car park.

Maisie and Gloria had thoroughly enjoyed the trip around

41

the pottery, as had Maurice. He was by now quite happy, having bought a little butter dish (reasonably priced though it was a 'second'), to sit in the sunshine and watch the town go by. Gloria assured him that they would be back soon and off they went to find a coffee bar before hitting the shops.

There were plenty of coffee bars to choose from—it was just a question of which one. They eventually chose one whose coffee aromas drew them irresistibly through the door. The décor was pretty much in keeping with French bad taste: gaudy, gold-framed, high-backed chairs with fuchsia-pink oilcloths on the tables; bare wood flooring and a high tidy bar backed with large mirrors and trimmed with the usual selection of spirits and adverts for *Noilly Prat* and *Ricard*. The former was a long-standing source of amusement for Eddie who several years previously had spent most of his first week in France informing Denis at every appropriate opportunity or even just for the hell of it that he was, a 'Noily prat'—an "Oily prat". This was preceded by him laughing uproariously at his own humour.

On top of the polished bar was the ubiquitous Stella pump and a huge coffee machine from which was emanating the irresistible odour which had drawn them in. Finding a seat in the corner, they sat waiting for Mr Patron to come over and take their order.

It wasn't long before the bronzed, slightly-on-the-wrong-side-of-his-forties bar-steward came slithering across,

"Ah bonjour, mesdames," he said welcomingly, and, before he had the chance to continue, Maisie said in a voice loud enough to compensate for the fact that he was foreign,

"We are English."

It sounded more like an announcement than a remark, which is often the way that English people abroad tend to address the locals, declaring their nationality as though it should engender a gasp and a deep bow of courtesy to follow.

"Ah Eeenglish," he said with a huge twinkle in his eye directed at the gals, whilst at the same time his other eye did the continental surveillance routine that wasn't wasted on either Maisie or Gloria and elicited embarrassed giggles from them both.

"'Ow can I make you 'appy?" he enquired, subtly continuing the continental mating ritual, pretending cutely that he didn't know how else to put it. Both girls swallowed the bait whole, giggling across at each other and thinking, "What a sweetie!"

Olivier, for that was his name, was warming up nicely.

"Deux cafés au laits, please, er, s'il vous plaît," responded Maisie.

"And can I get you tart, ladies?" he enquired.

With more juvenile giggling, the gals quickly put off the diet for another day and ordered two large fruit-filled meringues which the friendly Olivier was only too happy to slink over with, making sure that he leaned across each of them in turn whilst serving the other the sugary sweet. "Yum yum," drooled Maisie innocently, which Olivier, true to form, took the wrong way and fairly skipped back to his little lair behind the counter. Maisie and Gloria, oblivious to the 'innocents abroad' role that they were playing out, slurped their frothy coffees and munched their way through the two large meringues. Like two school girls they continued to target badly disguised, furtive glances at Olivier who, with an exaggerated flourish, continued to dry the same glass several times.

Gloria, who had managed to get most of the insides of her French pastry on her face and fingers, excused herself, and went off to the powder room, partially to clean up but, more importantly, to touch up the old war paint. As she slipped past the counter she flashed a particularly subtle free smile in the direction of Olivier and slipped into the ladies.

When she returned, Maisie had gone, so too had Olivier. As Gloria's fruit meringue gently somersaulted in her stomach, the artificial bamboo curtain which led into the back of the café shimmered and through it stepped a small, rather agitated, elderly, moustachioed man who looked far more like a patron than a gigolo, and, believing Gloria had just walked in, said in a brusque voice, "Oui, Madame?"

Gloria, struggling to remain calm, not one of her strengths, spluttered something that a trained ear would have found unintelligible, thus giving the patron no chance. He gave a Gallic shrug and carried on re-arranging glasses. Gloria grabbed her bag and fell out of the café, snagging her heel on the way out and dragging the *Bien Venue* mat out into the street behind her.

Screaming hysterically several times at the offending article to "get off!" ensured that by the time she had finally managed to shake it off she had attracted the attention of several other Gallic shruggers.

After some distance, Gloria's initial panic had subsided from hysteria into a more fearful state with concern accompanied by a tinge of envy at the idea that her bosom buddy had managed apparently to disappear with the bronzed Olivier. She had the presence of mind to give a little bit of the benefit of the doubt to the episode, and decided to act as calmly as possible with regard to Maisie's absence, considering it, at least for a while, as more of a mystery than a disaster.

Unfortunately without Maisie's sense of direction, she did not have the presence of mind to find her way back to the car park and spent the next hour wandering the streets of Quimper, before remembering that the car park had been next to 'that big church'.

Without the security of Gloria's presence, Maisie's enjoyment of the flirtation had been dampened somewhat and she had tried to keep her head down and eyes fixed firmly on her coffee cup while awaiting her companion's return from the washroom. After a minute or so she had become aware of a presence at the table, and, looking up, there was Olivier with a little-boy-lost look across his face. He was muttering something about his pictures of the Lady Diana and his flashing statue whilst at the same time ushering Maisie into the back of the café.

"Ha ha," Maisie laughed nervously. "Where are you, Glo? Please come back…quick!"

Breathing deeply, she pulled herself together thinking, "I'm a big girl, he just wants me to look at his pictures—sweet." And getting up, making sure she didn't leave her bag behind, she followed him into the back.

In the back room Olivier wasted no time with his flashing effigies and, saying something about Maisie being his little princess and would she like him to "smurge 'er leepsteek", he made a lunge at her.

At that moment Monsieur le Patron, returning from a trip next door to borrow a cup of sugar or something, and irritated at finding the café unattended, burst through the bamboo curtain and began berating his feckless son for bringing home his paramours when he was meant to be watching the café.

"Allez! Allez!" he snapped at the bemused and mightily relieved Maisie who was already well and truly 'allezing' out of the café.

Not waiting to see if Gloria had finally finished in the powder room, and not really caring, she stumbled off at speed towards the car park. As she calmed down a bit a slight smile broke over her face.

"No damage done," she thought, and she had pulled— well, *hadn't she?*

By the time that Gloria had woven her way through Quimper's narrow streets to the car park, Maisie was already there. Leaning nonchalantly against the car, checking her nails she looked up and greeted her erstwhile companion:

"All right, Glo?" she said. "How d'ya get on?"

There was no answer to that one, thought Gloria, and didn't bother trying. She just smiled sweetly.

Poor Denis, who having got fed up of wandering around on his own and had been at the car park for a long time already, didn't understand the significance of the remark but was intrigued as to why they had come back separately. When he casually enquired as to where Granddad was, he was further intrigued to see Maisie and Gloria reunited and disappearing back out of the car park in the direction of the pottery works. When thirty minutes later they returned Maurice-less, he knew from their expressions that something was not right.

In the meantime Eddie had returned, and, with Denis's help, had already secreted his purchases in the back of the car; looking a little bit sheepish, at the same time he was desperately struggling to furnish a plausible excuse for his profligacy.

Following shortly after Eddie, a frothing Clare had appeared dragging a stropping Jack still determinedly clutching two chicken feathers. This rather pensive group of 'tourists', each lost in their own thoughts, leaned against the car awaiting the return of the missing Maurice.

An hour later, just as they had reluctantly decided that the 'Granddad's out' plan, i.e. everybody to scour Quimper, would have to be initiated, strolling into the car park, accompanied by a late middle-aged bird on each arm, came Maurice.

Kissing him affectionately on each cheek before bidding, "Au revoir, Maureece," the two ladies ambled away, faces beaming. Maurice, a tin of home-made Breton biscuits in one hand, a bottle of locally distilled Calvados in the other, was, from deaf ear to deaf ear, also beaming.

"What a guy!" chuckled Denis. "What a guy!"

It was a rather subdued party that sat around the remnants of the barbecue that evening, each one pondering the day's events. Denis whose day had been uniquely uneventful proffered the first little teaser.

"How did you get on today, Clare? Anything interesting happen?"

"Not really," said Clare, the late evening's gloom hiding her bright red blushes.

"How about you girls, get up to anything interesting?"

"You'd better ask Shirley Valentine," snapped Gloria icily.

"Goodnight, Denis," responded Maisie, disappearing into the tent before Denis had time to continue.

Shortly after retiring, the screams from the tent next door alerted Denis to the fact that Eddie had decided that honesty was probably a preferable alternative to trying to keep a ten-foot long fishing rod hidden for another two weeks. Eventually the noise subsided and Denis lay staring out of the open tent flap, pondering the enormity of the universe and the significance of Maisie's sudden exit to bed.

He drifted off to sleep with a question niggling away in his head.

"Who the hell was Shirley Valentine?"

Chapter Four

The great thing about summer rain is that it rarely falls for two consecutive days and, true to form, next day as the morning's sunshine hit the back of the tents, the happy campers were awoken by that pleasantly unpleasant feeling that they were slowly suffocating in their sleeping bags.

Just as the heat build-up in the tent, caused by the carefully battened down windows and flaps, reached a critical level, Denis managed to locate the zip in the hermetically sealed plastic window and fling it open. The relatively cool air hitting him full in the face shocked him into life. Denis was one of those people who, when they are awake, they are awake. Springing, as best he could while entwined in a sleeping bag, he let out his excited and seriously irritating "Yabba dabba doo!" shocking almost all of the rest of the camp out of their slumbers and evoking an exasperated,

"Denis, do you have to?" from Maisie.

Denis, who could not then resist the lure of his juvenile sense of humour, proceeded to struggle over Maisie's slumbering body making sure that he caused maximum annoyance by catching her in the face with his knee, as he clambered out.

"Denis, you are so sad!" screamed Maisie, getting

seriously irritated with her childish husband, and helped him on his way by smashing her fist into his backside.

Zipping down the tent flap, Denis stepped outside and exaggeratedly sucked in a huge breath of cool morning air. Across in the meadow, through which, just the previous morning, a fairly large river had galloped along, there rose a silky sheet of early morning summer mist. The grass was sparkling with dew, soaking his feet, but Denis hardly noticed.

"Camping in France," he thought. "Wow."

Throwing both arms into the air, head back and legs astride, he looked into the sky and shouted at the top of his voice, "YES!"

It was 8.30.

"Oh Gawd! Denis is up," thought Eddie.

Unlike Denis, Eddie was not an instant waker and he had never quite come to terms with Denis's enthusiasm for early morning reveille but then again, neither had anybody else. The long-suffering, Maisie had even considered divorce as an option.

Unperturbed, Denis had soon put plan 'B' into operation. He knew that a cup of 'Rosie Lee' would convince the adults that surrendering with honour, helped along by a nice cup of tea, was far preferable to waiting for him to think up more and more irritating ways of letting them know it was time to get up.

He had once, whilst 'camping à la ferme' with Maisie, chucked a live chicken onto her bed to encourage her to rise. It had worked but he only did it the once!

Just as he was putting the kettle on the gas, along strolled Granddad returning from his early morning ablutions.

"Good morning, Maurice," greeted Denis enthusiastically.

"Isn't it just?" replied Maurice with a twinkle.

Denis, chuckling to himself, put the kettle on. It wasn't long before the screech of the whistle convinced Eddie et al that the night was indeed over but they also knew that if they waited a while before appearing they would get a bit of room service from the impatient Denis and indeed they did.

After the wake-up drink, out they all shuffled in various states of wakefulness and began to get ready for the one thing that sunny weather in France meant, and that was the beach. Tea in bed didn't really work with Clare so Denis had to resort to the more subtle approach of dragging her out by her feet.

Somewhere in the bundled-up sleeping bag was Jack, who having grown tired of jumping on Clare at around 7.30, had fallen back to sleep again. Clare, as usual, didn't believe what her dad had done but then again she hadn't been believing for years.

By the time everybody was up and about, the sun had well and truly begun to climb in the sky, leaving the trees that skirted Monique's property well behind. By this point, the temperature was reaching immobility level, where it starts to become a more attractive option to sit down than to clamber around in stuffy tents getting ready for the beach. Though this languorous approach to the day was one of the attractions of the outdoor holiday, it also meant that things don't really get going until around lunch-time. In fact, by the time the girls had finished their preparations, being ready by lunchtime was quite an achievement.

Breakfast had been, as usual, very much a makeshift effort, drinks of coffee or hot chocolate, very dry bits of baguette with jam or honey and the good old 'BN' biscuits. Jack was totally happy filling his mouth with anything that was on offer and Maisie made sure that he had plenty of bread and honey and lots to drink because of the heat. Clare, as usual, found most of what was on offer unappetising apart from the BN biscuits, which she managed to finish off.

At long last, everybody was ready and the majority of the things which they might need on the beach had been stuffed into the back of the car. Jack had made sure that all of his beach things were included—he loved the beach. Maurice decided that his desire for entertainment had been fully satiated by the previous day's excitement, so leaving him sitting in the shade of a large horse chestnut tree, with a hanky on his head, they set off for the coast.

Brittany's famous pink granite coast was the destination to which they were heading and the resort of Tregestel was the beach that offered the best facilities for everyone. On the way there they stopped at a *hypermarché* near Lannion to pick up lunch.

"It won't take a minute," reassured Maisie, to stem Clare's flow of grumbles, but of course, it did. This was actually because of Clare herself deciding that she needed the toilet, and then getting into an argument with Jack (one which she couldn't hope to win), who insisted that he too needed the toilet. She, of course, would have to accompany him and when they got there he refused to go in where the girls go and demanded she take him into the boys' toilet. She tried to explain that she could not go into the men's toilet, though being in France she could probably have got away with it. Eventually after a huge tantrum, she had to drag him back to the car without either of them having been because she couldn't leave him outside on his own and he wouldn't budge.

The adults, for whom the heat of the car was beginning to drain their will to live, were mightily relieved to see them return, Clare, however, who still hadn't been relieved, insisted that she needed to go back as did her little brother. So as he trudged his way back to the shopping mall accompanying Jack, it was Denis's turn to mutter Clare's usual lament of "I don't believe it!"

When they got there, Jack decided that he didn't need to go after all but could he have a drink? By the time Clare returned, it was a very subdued little boy she found sitting in the back of the car, Denis having brought the episode to a close by applying some old-fashioned psychology.

Clare realising that she couldn't get into the toilet without a coin had actually returned for some money but it didn't take a sixth sense to interpret the atmosphere in the car and realise that the better option was to sit cross-legged for the rest of the journey. So as the car pulled away from the *intermarché* car park, the best part of an hour had passed and squirming in the back was Clare.

"I really do not believe this," she thought.

When they eventually arrived at the car park, opposite the beach, it was nearly one o'clock. Clare hardly waited for the car to stop before stumbling off looking for the toilet. The others could hardly wait to escape from the baking car, and, as quickly as possible, struggling with Jack, and all of his beach equipment, crossed the road between the car-park and the beach. As well as Jack's things they carried their own beach gear, camping chairs, mats, towels, swimming gear, inflatable dinghy, bags with magazines, suntan cream, after-sun, drinks, cups, and, of course, the day's provisions, collected at the stop on the way.

It didn't take them too long to decide on a spec for the day and, curiously, because of the habit of the locals of not arriving on the beach until well after the noon hour, the beach was relatively quiet. There was, therefore, a surfeit of prime real estate from which to choose, but struggling across soft sand in temperatures in the eighties meant that a place, fairly close to the entrance to the beach, was as good a place as any, and they wasted no time in staking a claim to their own patch.

Eagerly setting out their towels, et cetera, they quickly settled to their respective beach activities. Maisie and Gloria, greased up like two well basted turkeys with pre-sun, during the sun, after sun and everything under the sun, lay down for some serious cooking. Eddie and Denis sat on the edge of their respective towels surveying the scene.

One of the first noticeable differences about a French beach, which sets it apart from its British counterpart, other than the fact that it remains relatively empty until after noon hour and that it isn't raining or blowing a gale, are the topless bathers. As much as possible, Denis and Eddie averted their eyes, both as a mark of respect and staunch loyalty to their other halves, and crucially because of the fact that they didn't fancy having their eyes gouged out without anaesthetic. Despite this, they always seemed to park themselves in such a position so that a high proportion of the beach's most attractive topless bathers were located within easy view. Wherever they turned, it seemed, yet another blissfully unaware young nymph would be gently bouncing up the beach towards them, unwittingly distracting them from thoughts of their snoring wives sizzling gently beside them. When a group of young things actually came and parked themselves right next to them, that was as much as they could cope with.

"I'm off for a swim," said Eddie, and plodded off towards the cool blue water.

Actually, after the burning temperatures of the beach, the cool blue water did indeed seem very inviting. Unfortunately, having left his mat in a bit of a hurry, Eddie had left his protective flip flops behind and, after a few steps, completed the short distance to the water hopping from one burnt foot to the other, accompanied by very loud 'Hoo-hah, hoo-hahs'.

The 'hoo-hahs' attracted the attention of a bunch of local boys who, fascinated at the sight of this large, milk-white, obviously foreign lump of lard in floral Bermuda shorts, dancing his way to the edge of the tide, were distracted from their horseplay at the water's edge.

As is the nature of hot days on the beach, despite the very enticing appearance of the blue sea, the level of the body temperature relative to that of the water means that getting in the water is far more difficult than it at first appears.

Making his way cautiously into the sea, the 'hoo-hahs' continued, though this time for slightly different reasons, but he was actually doing fine. Having just reached the critical point when the legs are nicely acclimatised and it's time to bite the bullet for the tricky bits, Eddie was just thinking that, as with ripping off a plaster, it was best just to do it quickly, when one of the little boys who were beginning to swarm around him, thoroughly enjoying his performance, decided to help him take the plunge. He launched himself into the water behind the tentative bather, causing a huge spout of water to land on his hot back. The sudden shock caused Eddie to lose his balance and down he went, straight under the salty surf.

By the time he had managed to restore his equilibrium and stand up again, Eddie who did not previously suffer from asthma, thought that he was having his first attack. He did, however, soon recover and, thinking positively, decided that, as he was happy at having the usually tortuous process rushed along, the boys had actually done him a favour.

Believing that the best way to deal with his newfound *friends* was to give the impression that all was fine and dandy, he forced a laugh and splashed out at the nearest one to him, as if encouraging the game. Bad move, Eddie: the best course of action would have been to ignore them! Appearing to join in the game had the little horrors slobbering with glee and they immediately responded with a torrent of excited hoots of delight and a cascade of icy splashes in Eddie's direction. Eddie didn't generally mind the odd splash about but the force of the barrage of water which hit him took his breath away and he began to flounder around, trying to get out of range. Unfortunately, in a similar way to predatory sharks, his thrashing about had attracted all the little rascals in the immediate area and he was soon surrounded by a crowd of excited French kids who were beginning to reach a level of hysteria that was positively worrying.

In his desperation, Eddie decided to splash back, believing that this would provide a clear tunnel through which he could escape. Winding up his arm, he spun around and went to hit the water but misjudged, slapping the nearest boy in the ear. That's when all hell broke loose.

The good news was that the splashing stopped immediately, the bad news that it was replaced with a piercing scream. The good news continued when the boys around him disappeared with amazing speed followed by the bad news that the attention of just about every other bather in the area was directed at Eddie. Trying to make amends, Eddie attempted to reach out to the hysterical youngster but, just at the moment he put a reassuring arm around his victim's head, the little wretch pulled away and they both plunged headlong into the tide, Eddie landing heavily on top of the boy. By the time they reappeared most of the beach, including the victim's family, were converging on Eddie. Contemplating the difficulties involved in attempting to explain away this unfortunate chain of events, which had culminated in the apparent assault and attempted drowning of one of his tormentors, Eddie took a huge breath and disappeared under the water. Putting as much distance as possible between him and the pursuing pack, before surfacing behind a large piece of pink granite was, he decided, the discretion which was the better part of valour, so that is what he did.

Back on the beach, Denis was still sitting surveying the scene. Not a great one for sun worshipping Denis tended to get his suntan incidentally, much preferring to observe the goings-on around than to lie stretched out at the mercy of its burning rays.

"What's that noise all about, Denis?" asked Maisie, turning herself over to do the other side.

"There's something going on in the sea. A whole bunch of people milling round, splashing and shouting. It must be some sort of group activity. Amazing people, the French," he mused, "they're so community-spirited."

"You can't see Eddie, can you, Denis?" Gloria enquired. "He's been gone a long time."

"Nah, he's probably right in the middle of the mêlée having a great time."

The large piece of pink granite behind which Eddie was concealed and onto which he was clinging was beginning to cut into his knees and fingers. As well as the discomfort inflicted by the sharp rock, Eddie's upper torso was baking in the sun whilst at the same time his lower half was beginning to feel the cold as the warmer water of the shallows was being slowly replaced, bit by bit by the incoming tide. His rock of refuge would soon be under water and Eddie would either become exposed from his hiding place or submerged with it.

As Denis had correctly surmised Eddie was well and truly 'in the middle of it' but it wasn't the word 'mêlée' which best described what he was in the middle of.

"Come on, kids," invited Denis. "Let's go and get the dinghy in the sea and paddle to those rocks."

Clare, who by now was heartily sick of Jack destroying every one of her attempts at sand sculpture, was quite happy to join her dad in the inflatable. Jack, as usual, was game for anything but insisted on taking his bucket and spade with them in case they met any sharks. It didn't make a lot of sense but Jack could be pretty determined when he wanted to be and, like most children, would not leave go of an idea which he had thought up on his own. Denis knew that he would have to give in eventually and that resistance was really just putting off the inevitable. Anyway, it was no big deal except that Clare was making out that it was but only because she considered Jack was a spoilt brat who always got his own way. Jack had slipped into 'if you think this is a scene you ain't seen nothing yet' mode and the argument would have carried on if Maisie hadn't intervened.

"Oh for goodness sake, just take him, will you!" she yelled.

"Okay, okay," returned Denis. "Just let me get my bathers on."

Denis grabbed a towel and girded himself with it before doing the precarious 'wriggle wriggle' dance to extricate himself from his shorts and pants. Rooting through one of the beach bags Denis found the black trunks that Maisie had bought for him just the other day in Quimper. As soon as he pulled the packet out of the bag alarm bells began to tinkle and when he took them out of the plastic wrapping and saw the picture of the bloke on the front sporting them, the bells were well and truly clanging. The picture showed a muscular Adonis whose body was dominated by two buttocks up which was disappearing a strip of black cloth.

"Bloody hell, Maisie you've bought me a thong!"

"Oh just get on with it, Denis, for goodness sake, this is Europe, it's twenty-first century France, anyway that's all they had...apart from in leopard skin!" she added mischievously.

At this point Gloria began a giggle, which was still going on some ten minutes later.

"No one's going to see you between here and the sea and anyway do you think they'll notice? They all wear skimpies."

Denis, muttering away, managed to slide into the trunks and, pulling hard in order to stretch the back of the garment to cover as much of himself as possible, was almost breaking the stitches. At the same time Clare and the girls *were* in stitches.

So off they went to the water's edge to launch the ship which would take them off to a paradise island. As he walked along, Denis, much to the disappointment of Maisie and Gloria, placed the paddle strategically behind him to save his modesty; once in the water he was safe.

It was a little bit cramped in the boat especially with Jack's accompanying bucket, spade and rake. As they got under way, Denis was well in his element close to the shore but as they moved off further from the beach and towards the 'island' he began to become aware of their vulnerability. As the bottom fell away quickly the clear blue water had become quite dark and ominous, and Denis was beginning to feel a little nervous. Whilst Clare and Jack were urging him on towards the island, Denis was beginning to realise the difficulty there is in being able to judge distances across flat surfaces and was aware that the island in fact was still some considerable distance away. The kids, loving every moment, weren't aware of their dad's discomfort and neither were they aware of the reason for it.

The problem was Denis didn't swim too well, in fact to be perfectly accurate, Denis could only swim safely on his back and, only then, short distances because every time he tried to turn to see where he was going, he would roll over, panic and start to sink. Sinking in the relative safety of a swimming pool is one thing, sinking in the middle of the English Channel is something quite different. Still he put on a brave face and smiled with pretended enthusiasm as the kids unhampered by any sense of danger shouted, "Faster, faster!"

Denis, noticeably flagging under the heat of the sun, responded gamely, paddling a bit faster and before too long the island, which was actually a huge rock, was only about ten metres away.

"Thank God for that," thought Denis. "Now all we have to do is get back."

It was at this point that Jack, having tired of being in the back of the boat, decided that he would be the first ashore and began to make his way to the front, no easy task in a small inflatable dinghy. Before he could take his second step, Denis, like some demented Barbara Woodhouse, shouted, "SIT!!"

Even Jack was taken aback by the power of the command and would have sat down immediately anyway but Denis was already up himself to make sure that he did. Unfortunately, as he stood up he put his bare foot onto the spikes of Jack's rake, let out an agonised scream and fell out of the dinghy. By the time he surfaced, he was halfway between the dinghy and the rock.

"Oh great," he thought. "Bloody great."

He managed, eventually, to direct himself back to the boat but, as his first attempt to climb back on board almost resulted in the whole thing tipping over, he soon realised that the chances of safely achieving that particular objective, as well as being less than slim, were also very dangerous. The boat, carried by the tide, was in fact drifting slowly away from the rock and Denis realised if he couldn't get into it he'd have to cling on. Unfortunately, wherever he clung, his weight pulled down the side of the vessel and water started to pour in. This resulted in Clare screaming uncontrollably, as Jack, seeing no danger, laughed uproariously and swung round at his dad with his spade shouting, "Get away! You bad pirate!"

As the rock began to drift further and further away, Denis realised that he would, after all, have to trust his ability to float in the right direction and headed for the safety of the island to regroup.

"Just keep paddling, Clare," he shouted, "the tide will take you to the beach."

"I don't believe this," moaned Clare and began to paddle.

After a while, when his head smacked against the rock, Denis realised that he had reached his goal. Fortunately, he had been aware of this possibility so he had been progressing with appropriate caution. Several attempts later Denis managed to scramble up on to its relative safety.

The euphoria of having achieved his first objective soon evaporated as the question arose, "So what now, Denis, mate?"

Reassured to see in the distance Clare and Jack making steady progress towards the shore, he decided not to panic just yet and gave them a wave but they didn't respond. Jack was having far too much fun and Clare wasn't really in the mood to wave back. Denis's immediate concern was that the protection offered by the less than all-embracing swimming trunks was far from adequate and the sharp pink granite was giving his bare bottom hell; there was no real escape from this as the rest of his body was equally exposed. He was just considering slipping back into the water for a bit of relief when he heard someone call his name.

"Oh God," he thought, "I'm delirious." And then he remembered once seeing a film where the hero had actually died and life had apparently carried on as normal and he hadn't realised he was in fact dead until the end. He was just coming to terms with the reality that he had drowned after falling out of the dinghy when he heard his name again.

"Denis, Denis, it's me, Eddie!"

Out from behind an adjacent rock popped Eddie, looking slightly embarrassed and at the same time grinning inanely and very pleased to see his pal Denis.

"What you doing here?" he asked, rather predictably.

"Trying out my new bathers," replied Denis sarcastically.

"Mm, very nice," said Eddie.

So there they both were, perched on one large piece of granite. Eddie, able to swim but unable to return to a charge of common assault and attempted murder by drowning, and Denis unable to swim.

"Oh Gawd," thought Eddie.

"Bloody Hell," thought Denis.

Jack was just getting to appreciate the role of sea captain and was enjoying even more lauding it over his bossy sister, who had been paddling away like his little slave, when they reached the shore. She in turn had tired of Jack's attitude problem way before they hit the beach so she rather peevishly gave a quick jerk on the rope as she pulled the boat up out of the water and dumped Jack out of the back and into the shallow surf.

"You're so sad," he said as he struggled up, mimicking his mother's usual observation of his dad. "And you're stupid, and I hate you," he added for good measure.

" And you are a brat, so shut it and get a life, ya big baby," Clare responded gleefully, and off they trudged up the beach.

When they reached base camp Maisie and Gloria were just about to start getting the picnic ready.

"Just in time," Maisie greeted them. "Where's your dad?"

"Dunno, somewhere out there," said Clare, waving her arms vaguely in the direction of the English Channel.

"Is there anything to eat?"

"You haven't seen Eddie, have you, Clare?" asked Gloria.

"He's been gone ages."

"Nah," said Clare helpfully.

"Don't worry, Glo, they can't be up to much. Knowing Denis they'll be in a bar somewhere sitting in front of two cold Stellas."

"Not the way Denis was dressed when he left here," reminded Gloria, reducing them all to fits of giggles.

It was decision time out at sea. The two men were feeling the effects of too much sun on bare backs and needed to come up with a solution, fairly rapidly, before they died of sunstroke.

The other equally pressing reason was that the island, which Denis and the kids had originally headed for had by now been reduced to a somewhat smaller rock and, as the tide continued its steady rise, was barely big enough for the two men to fit comfortably on. Denis was once again excavating the thin strip of cloth from between his cheeks in an effort to prevent further lacerations to his bottom and Eddie was beginning to accept that he would just have to swim for it and face the consequences, when a boat appeared. Now this is the point in an adventure when the sleek, flashy yacht glides into view and the crew—young, slim, bikini-clad females—beckon our heroes on board for an afternoon of champagne and...well, that's not quite how it was.

The boat, a rather old fishing boat, was captained by a fisherman of similar age, weatherbeaten, ruddy faced, dressed in a striped shirt with a cigarette sticking out of the corner of his mouth, looking every inch the old salt he was. Eddie and Denis, balancing precariously and too ecstatic at seeing possible redemption to care less who was piloting the boat, stood up and let out a mixture of waves, cheers and shouts, towards their perceived saviour and over he came. By the time they had scrambled on board the vessel and looked back, the rock had disappeared completely.

The two of them slumped onto the bottom of the boat, too relieved to think about what would happen next. This was just as well really because as they lay there, imagining that they were heading back to the beach, the little boat was heading for the nearest jetty several miles in the other direction. It was only when Denis peered over the side to see how close they were that he realised the awful truth.

"Plage! Plage!" he cried vainly over the noise of the engine, at the old sea captain who, whilst carrying on in the direction of the distant jetty, grinned and called back,

"Oui, oui, la plage, c'est magnifique, eh?"

"Tell him we need the beach," said Eddie, with panic in his voice.

"I have done," Denis protested.

"He doesn't seem to understand, he probably only speaks Breton."

"Oh Gawd!" thought Eddie. "This is a nightmare."

The two castaways couldn't bring themselves to imagine the consequences of being dumped on the jetty miles from the beach and they didn't need to because in a short time they had arrived. Like two young squaddies waiting to go over the top, they were peering over side of the boat and into the abyss when the boat gently pulled alongside the stone steps of the quay.

And so, picture the scene as they set off on the long walk back to base camp, two radiantly pink, semi-naked men, stumbling out of the boat and on to the wharf: one wearing bright floral Bermudas, the other hardly covering his modesty, nothing but a tea bag held loosely in place by a thin shard of string, which intermittently disappeared from view. Even in liberal France, where beachwear is optional, the sight of the two men caused quite a stir—particularly as they had come ashore on market day thus dashing any hopes of discreetly blending into the background. Instead Eddie and Denis had to run the gauntlet of a corridor of busy stalls. The merchandise which was on view to the potential customers was nothing compared with what was passing before their eyes in the shape of our two heroes and conversations were punctuated with a stream of 'ooh la las' from locals, shaking their heads and making exaggerated hand gestures.

At the same time, fellow fishermen were engaged in animated conversation with their rescuer along the lines of, "What bait did you use to land this fine pair, ho ho ho?"

And so, despite their best efforts to cause as little to-do as possible as they set off on their long trek, they left in their wake quite a stir, having brightened up the generally mundane lives of the whole community.

It was four in the afternoon. The heat of the sun had turned the pavement into something resembling a griddle and as it continued to beat down Eddie and Denis, trying to look as inconspicuous as one can in the circumstances, were very quickly beginning to lose any semblance of normality as their feet, literally, began to bake.

The two men, leaning heavily on each other's shoulders, were, like two giant toads walking in huge strides, struggling vainly to keep going. As the pain in their feet became unbearable, they soon realised that they could not continue unless they did something about it. Just as they were leaving the last of the inhabited buildings which nestled around the small port, they spied a large municipal rubbish bin overflowing with the abandoned flotsam and jetsam of market day.

The first thing they dragged out was a huge piece of cardboard, which had once been a box. This provided Denis with enough material to restore some of his modesty. Wrapping the cardboard around his nether regions, he managed to cover most of his upper torso and his offending swimwear. Eddie more concerned about his back and chest, which were now red raw, found a black bin-bag, full of bottles. Having relieved it of its contents, he made it into a rather fetching jacket by ripping holes for his head and his arms. With his floral Bermudas poking out of the bottom, he would not have looked out of place on the catwalks of gay Paris.

They then fashioned a couple of sun hats out of two carrier bags and, using some string, fastened the handles under their chins. With these in place, all that was left was the footwear. In terms of reaching their destination this was the most important and proving the most difficult to improvise. They had enough string to tie up some thick corrugated cardboard for Eddie and then they struck lucky, well half-lucky: down in the bottom of the bin was a pair of old flip-flops. Unfortunately, these had been dumped because the strap of one of them had completely snapped off. Denis put the other one on, which Eddie eyed enviously, and then he found an old tissue box, which just fitted his other foot. In their enthusiastic search through the rubbish they had scattered litter far and wide and as they turned around, pleased with their resourcefulness and faces beaming, they spotted two very indignant French ladies one of whom began to berate loudly the two foreign hooligans. Ranting and raving at them, she left them in no doubt as to her feelings about their behaviour, ending her stream of abuse by pointing at her head and at the same time shouting,

"Fou! Fou!"

Eddie had just about had it: he was in the latter stages of sunstroke, his feet were melting and his back blistering. He had already suffered enough at the hands of the French for one day and 'entente cordial' was just not on his mind.

"Piss off!" he yelled with feeling, whilst for good measure giving the famous continental 'up yours' sign. The two ladies' mouths fell open and they lifted their skirts and hurried off to get away from the two dangerous lunatics.

"Assault and battery, attempted murder and now threatening behaviour towards two senior citizens. Nice one, Eddie," thought Denis, to whom the sanctuary of his little cosy bed, in his little tent trailer on the little campsite, seemed a million miles away.

So off they trudged, the Earnest Shackleton, and Captain Scott of the great outdoors heading for their distant goal equipped with all the specialist equipment of modern technology that a rubbish bin could provide. The rigid nature of the box on Denis's foot meant that stepping from heel to toe proved very difficult, nay impossible, so looking very much like a one-legged cross-country skier, he glided along on one foot while flopping along with the other. At least they were making progress and were soon leaving the mayhem of the jetty behind them. They were in fact beginning to feel quite upbeat and getting along very well; indeed, had it been physically possible, they would have had quite a spring in their step. It was then that the police car drew up beside them.

Back on the beach, Clare and Jack having been re-fuelled with a bounteous picnic were scrambling through rock pools searching for specimens. Rock-pooling was one of the few beach activities Clare and Jack could share without too much falling out; in addition, it gave Clare the chance to encourage Jack to fall into the water and, being a four-year-old, nothing suited Jack better.

"I wonder where they are," said Gloria, referring to their errant husbands. "They've been gone ages. I hope they're all right."

As she scanned the beach, her gaze stopped at the sight of two men flexing their bronzed, if somewhat less than youthful torsos down by the water's edge. They were surveying the scene apparently in search of potential 'totty'.

"Oh look," giggled Gloria, "That bloke's trunks are almost as skimpy as Denis's, and I'm sure I've seen him before," she added to herself. Maisie looked down towards the sea and the moment she spotted the two men her stomach turned; she knew exactly where she had seen one of them before—in a café in Quimper.

Pulling her sunhat well down over her face, she stared down at the sand.

"Ooh they're looking this way, Maise. Now they're smiling and nudging each other."

Gloria, preening herself, stared back and smiled.

"Maisie, they're coming this way! Now you just watch this, Maisie," she said as she turned around to her friend, but Maisie was already halfway up the beach on her way to the car park.

Gloria's excitement knew no bounds for walking straight towards her came the bronzed Olivier and his companion. Sitting up straight, her hair flung back and her bosom thrust forward, she postured shamelessly as the two men approached, and approached, and approached, and approached and...arrived...and walked straight past to join a group of young people further up the beach in a game of volley ball. At that point Clare and Jack came bouncing back looking for more food.

"Where's Mum?" said Clare.

"I've no idea!" snapped Gloria. "Get your things, we're going."

"Where's Dad and Eddie?" continued Clare, suggesting that they couldn't really go anywhere until they came back.

"I've no idea!"

"Wow-wee," thought Clare. "Who's been in the sun too long?"

As she began to collect up hers and Jack's things, her mother appeared sheepishly down some steps further along the wall at the edge of the beach. Spying that the coast was clear she had made her way back to the others from the opposite direction.

"I'll kill those two idiots when they get back," she said.

Gloria already had part of Eddie's anatomy roasting on an open fire.

So they all struggled off the beach with all their gear back to the car park and they all sat in the car awaiting the return of the two men. Had the men arrived at that point, death would probably have swiftly followed.

Inspector Bien and Special Constable La Gal had spent the whole of this very hot summer's day cooped up in their four-wheeled cooker. They had also spent the last hour bemoaning that the fates had decreed that their role in life should be to police long expanses of Brittany's pink granite coast where the last incident of any note had been the threatened invasion of Europe in 1944. Even this had never materialised, the unreliable allies having chosen the more upmarket, sandy beaches of Normandy. On sighting Eddie and Denis their spirits rose—they were not about to give this opportunity up lightly.

"Bonjour, bonjour, bonjour," greeted Inspector Bien.

"You are on your way to the carnival, yes?"

"We are English," Eddie offered apologetically.

"Oui, oui, that's right," butted in Denis, recognising the word 'carnival' and also being aware of the need to tread carefully, given the circumstances, not just the way in which they were attired but also Eddie's possible criminal record.

"Ah Eenglish, you are Eenglish," he repeated.

"David Beckham, Arsenal, Chelsea, Mr Blair...mad cows, roast beefs. But the Carnival is that way."

Denis having felt optimistic on hearing the football

connections, suddenly realised, from the tone of the delivery, that careful diplomacy was what was required here and that citing Bobby Charlton was probably not the way forward.

"Shut up, Eddie," he said before poor Eddie had managed to piece together his response.

"Yes, we have been to the carnival and now we are going back to our wives who are on the beach at Tregestel," Denis said reassuringly to the two officers.

"Ah bon, but the carnival was yesterday," replied Special Constable La Gal.

Denis struggling hard to understand the policeman, picked out clearly enough the words 'carnival' and 'yesterday', and began to visibly flounder in his cardboard box. Given his limited vocabulary, the idea of attempting to tell the truth as to how they had arrived there was clearly not an option. It was however imperative that the gendarmes, who were enjoying watching the English man squirm, were provided with a feasible reason as to why himself and his companion were sullying 'La Belle France' by promenading along their beautiful coastline dressed in bin bags, cardboard boxes and paper-bag hats.

"Now here's a challenge," thought Denis.

"Yesterday we go to the carnival and we love France and its wine and its beer and its beautiful people and we drink some wine and beer and went in the parade. Then we drank some more wine and more beer and we have a beautiful time, singing and drinking at the carnival and then we fell asleep, and now we have to go back to our wives to explain."

At this point Denis made an exaggerated cut-throat gesture to illustrate the challenge ahead of explaining away their night on the tiles. The two policemen already being slowly won over by the flattery of France, its people and reference to its most famous export were in total empathy when it came to the 'explaining' bit. They both began to laugh and make knowing gestures, tapping their noses and mimicking the knife across the throat. Eddie clearly aware that the crisis was almost over joined in the general ribaldry and heartily slapped Denis on the back dislodging his cardboard tunic which fell to the ground, just enough to reveal his rosy cheeks. The policemen both stared in unison and at the same moment the car radio crackled into life.

"Oui, oui deux Anglais, lunatics…two old ladies… vandalised the municipal refuse bin…yes, we have them here now…oh yes, it's them all right."

Bundling them into the back of the car, paying no regard to the damage being done to their carefully constructed clothing, Denis and Eddie were swiftly driven back to the scene of the crime. There they were bundled out again and made to make reparations for their misdemeanour by clearing up the whole street. Protestations that they had been responsible for only half of the mess would, had they been understood, fallen on deaf ears.

When they had finished the task they spotted the two old ladies standing, arms folded, at the side of the road with looks of intense satisfaction spreading across their wizened faces.

"Allez, allez, messieurs and au revoir," bid the two gendarmes and something along the lines of 'and don't come back in a hurry'.

Eddie was just about to reply when Denis said, "Don't, Eddie."

So off they set again on their long trek back to the beach from where they had set off many hours ago. It was now six-thirty, their protective clothing had suffered badly from their recent exertions but by now, early evening, it was beginning to get chilly. Denis had abandoned his cardboard for a garbage bag wrapped around his loins and, importantly, they still had their footwear. They were also still free men which, considering Eddie's performance so far that day, was something to be grateful for.

It was eight-thirty and beginning to get a bit dusky when the two silhouetted figures appeared at the entrance to the car park. In the half-light, they looked like a pair of drunks stumbling along, supporting each other's weight. The shoes had long since lost their effectiveness and their feet long since most of their feeling.

"Right," said Gloria with a purpose, "you're dead, Eddie Lancaster."

In their haste to get to their quarry, Gloria and Maisie almost fell out of the car. Clare and Jack having exhausted themselves arguing had been fast asleep in the back.

"This should be good,' thought Clare, awakened by the sudden change in atmosphere. But as they approached their prey, the two women realised that all was not as they had thought. The two men's bodies were glowing in the gloom, their faces seriously bright red and their lips cracked.

"Oh Denis, what happened?" asked Maisie, showing genuine concern. "Water, water," moaned Denis.

"Water, water," echoed Eddie.

"Drink, drink, Clare, Clare get them a drink."

Clare who was a tad disappointed that the drama wasn't

unfolding quite as expected felt compensated a little bit by the appearance of her dad and Eddie. Trying hard to hide her amusement, she pulled out the picnic bag to get the drink bottle out. It was quite full, not with juice but with sea water and two mud skippers which Jack had had in his bucket and was supposed to have returned to the sea.

"Oh Jack, you idiot," thought Clare, but Jack was oblivious to all that was going on. He had had another great day, despite his bossy sister, and now he was enjoying the sleep of the just.

"Water, water," continued the men plaintively.

"We haven't got any, it's gone. Come on, we'll soon be back at the camp."

Struggling painfully into the car, the two men, despite third degree burns to most of their body, tried as best they could to get comfortable. Every bend in the road that caused movement and brought raw flesh into contact with anything else also brought howls of pain from the men. It seemed a very long journey back to the tents punctuated every so often with delirious cries of, "Water, water."

And in the darkness, having got over their initial shock, titters from the gals.

Gloria, especially after the return of Eddie and Denis, had been showing uncharacteristic concern for her dad, Maurice, who had been left to his own devices all day. She imagined that he would still be sitting under the tree where they had left him in the hot sunshine but by now he would be freezing cold in the darkness with wild animals nibbling at his feet. When they eventually pulled into the field, Maurice was just finishing off his third glass of *Cote de Rousillion*, a nice medium- to full-bodied number with a hint of cabernet. He was washing down the final morsels of some cote d'agneau, served in a rich creamy mushroom sauce accompanied by a selection of vegetables fresh from Monique's garden. He was, apparently, in no danger of succumbing to hypothermia or of being devoured by wild animals: in fact, though he couldn't hear or understand much of the conversation going on around him, Maurice was perfectly content. Sitting next to him, Monique's widowed mother was completely taken with the archetypal English gentleman at her side, and attending to his every need.

Unaware of Maurice's comfortable situation, there was a panic-ridden fifteen minutes of searching high and low for the missing Maurice, before Gloria, on her way to Monique's to ask if anyone had spotted him, spied him through the drapeless windows looking more than safe, and very happy.

Safe maybe but 'happy' was not a word that could be used to describe the rest of the party. Their usual stop-off at the *supermarché* on the way back from the beach had not happened due to the condition of Denis and Eddie who, shortly after arriving back, having rehydrated themselves, had gone to their respective beds. Though they hadn't eaten since breakfast, they were too exhausted and in too much pain to think about food. Coated from head to toe in calamine lotion they tried to sleep. Maisie and Gloria made some soup and found some reasonably fresh baguette which, unsurprisingly, was not fully appreciated by Clare and they all turned in fairly early.

The postscript to the day's events happened about four in the morning when Eddie needed to go to the toilet. As a result of a friend's experience, who, whilst answering the call of nature in the middle of the night, had inadvertently urinated on an electric fence, resulting in him being hospitalised for a week, Eddie, however late at night or early in the morning it was, always went to the toilet block. Eddie tramped off to Monique's house to use the bathroom and, finding it occupied when he got there, stood patiently waiting. When the door opened the sight that faced Monique's younger sister was Eddie white from head to toe in calamine lotion looking for all the world like a dreadful spectre. She immediately let out a piercing scream, which curdled the blood of everyone in hearing distance. Eddie, as frightened by her reaction as Lisette had been by the apparition, responded with a scream of his own which, back in the tent, woke Maisie up with a start. She flung her arms out, hitting Denis across his badly burnt frontage; he screamed in equal measure of terror and pain, waking Gloria up who herself had been sleeping fitfully as a result of mixed feelings of shame, concern for Eddie and guilt. On realising Eddie was missing she began to scream:

"Eddie! Eddie! Where's my Eddie?"

Clare lay in her sleeping bag not believing any of it while Maurice, with the hint of a smile on his face, continued his deep sleep. Being as deaf as a post wasn't all bad.

Chapter Five

The next few days could best be described as 'fallow' days. The sun continued to beat down which meant that it was wise to leave the tents early in the morning to avoid suffocation and after the excitement of that memorable day at the beach everyone was happy to laze around trying to keep, as far as possible, in the shade.

Denis and Eddie were not really in a fit state to go anywhere, having to have regular re-coats of After Sun, and, being typical men, whilst it was being applied, made the most of the suffering it involved. Maurice was quite content to promenade the local area with his latest companion, which, despite his pain, made Denis chuckle.

The adults spent the days lazing around for most of the time except that Maisie and Gloria did nip into town to do a bit of shopping for tea in the evening. Having brunched with Monique, they reciprocated the gesture at supper and were joined by Monique's family around the camping table. After struggling bravely, Eddie was proud to have prepared and presented parcels of julienne fish cooked in butter and various herbs and garlic, these being much appreciated by their French friends. Eddie would have much preferred it had he actually caught the fish himself with his newly acquired rod, but, after their ordeal in the sun, neither himself nor Denis were yet in a fit state of health to do anything other than potter around, generally feeling sorry for themselves, as men often do. Unable to move further than within the close proximity of the tent, they had to rely on Maisie and Gloria successfully identifying the correct species on the fish counter of the Crozon Intermarché. The fact that they did actually bring back the right goods was almost as surprising as Eddie landing a fish, so for the moment, anyway, he was satisfied with that.

The following evening, Eddie's gesture was reciprocated by the French group with a huge bowl of steaming mussels cooked in a white wine and cream sauce, again with garlic to help the flavour along. Denis started to produce some bouef hachées for the children, but had to abandon the efforts halfway through when his sensitive skin began to react to the heat of the barbecue and so Clare took over.

"Oh that is so gross!" said Clare when after two or three days, Eddie and Denis, like two reptiles, began to emerge slowly from their old skins as they started to peel off in ever-larger sheets. Beginning to feel a little more able to venture further than Monique's field it was decided that a spot of visiting was in order.

Neville and Bea Owen were two old friends of Denis and Maisie who eight years previously, around the time that their eldest child Jacob was about to start school, had decided that they had had enough of the rat race in England. Neville had packed in his job as a teacher in a large secondary school and they had sold up their house and fled to rural Brittany. Denis wasn't too sure exactly where they were but he did know that they were always very encouraging about visiting them and, after some searching through her bag, Maisie had found a telephone number.

On answering the phone, Bea was thrilled that someone from back home had made contact and enthused at the idea of them visiting: "Come tomorrow, come for lunch, we'll have a barbecue in the evening. The kids'll be thrilled."

It wasn't too difficult to find the house, which was close to the town of Sizun, and meant a trip back over the bridge. After driving along a small road off the main square for several miles it did not take long to locate 'chez Owen'. If by chance they had lost their way, the Owen kids would have ensured that they did not drive past.

There were five of them ranging in age from five to twelve. As they drove slowly down the lane from Sizun, the children came flying out of the driveway of the renovated house to which the Owens had given a strange, unpronounceable name...which was, apparently, Breton for 'Tranquillity'. This was a somewhat misleading title for the house as when the kids were around it was anything but tranquil.

Clare had not been too keen on the visit from the start as she still bore several scars, both physical and psychological, from her previous encounter with the little dears and gave an audible groan when she saw them appear. Neville and Bea, having escaped from the rat race, which they felt was slowly suffocating them, appeared to have embraced without reservation the 'good life'. In other words they had 'gone native' big time!

Stepping out of the shadow of an old semi-derelict barn

at the side of the old cottage appeared Neville, looking not dissimilar to *Treasure Island's* Ben Gunn. Dressed in a smock, knee-length breeches, and old heavy boots, he held out a welcoming hand to Denis, who was first to reach him, giving him a very limp handshake. Denis, still in a bit of a shock at the sight of his old buddy and his new image, was not quite sure how to respond and managed a,

"Hiya, Nev, good to see you, you're looking.... . How's Bea?"

"Cor blimey!" thought Eddie. "He's a bloody hippy!"

Maisie was equally taken aback by the appearance of Neville. The last time she had seen him he had been in a suit, shirt and tie, and carrying a briefcase. As she went to give him the customary greeting, he grabbed her enthusiastically, hugged her closely and gave her the traditional kisses on each cheek—two on this occasion, as was demanded in this particular area of Brittany. The closeness of the hug brought her into immediate proximity to an odour which was a mixture of garlic, tobacco, fish and general bodily secretions which rather smothered her attempts to utter,

"Good to see you, Neville." And it came out as more of a "'Guh! Neville."

Neville had truly embraced rural Brittany, indeed, he smelt as if he had recently been rolling in it.

Gloria was, well, Gloria, to be fair, had been a late arrival on the camping scene and, though she did try to put her heart into it for Eddie's sake, and loved many aspects of the great outdoors, she still relied heavily on her creature comforts. Things like clean clothes, a place to shower and do one's hair and nails had never really became superfluous on Gloria's list of 'must have availables'. So the sight of Neville closely followed by a rather subservient-looking Bea, did not fill her with any sense of envy or admiration for two people who had left the rat race behind. In fact her immediate response, under her breath of course, was "Yuck!" "Nice to meet you," said Gloria, greeting first Neville and then Bea with the same strangled-at-birth enthusiasm.

"France is lovely, isn't it?" she stammered, trying to display at least a little solidarity with their obvious love affair with the rural part of their host country.

As soon as Jack and Clare had alighted from the car, the Owen children had made a beeline for Jack and whisked him off to goodness-knows-where. A previously absent sense of protection arose in Clare and, having already suffered enough at their hands, was not about to allow her suddenly beloved brother out of her sight. There were of course times when she could have happily strangled Jack but it is amazing how family loyalties can melt the hardest of hearts and he was, after all, her brother and the only one she had.

Setting off in hot pursuit, she was just in time to see the kids disappearing around the corner of the building, through a back door and into the barn itself. As she appeared they seemed to have been surprised to see her but quickly regained their composure and greeted her warmly. Clare was not at all fooled and wondered what they were up to. Last time it was, disappear for half an hour, re-appear with Jack painted blue having used only the best blackberry juice squeezed from fresh blackberries picked from the hedgerows which bordered the English lanes. Apart from being slightly irritated by the retinue of flies attracted by the sweet juice, buzzing around his head, Jack thought it was great being blue and was far more irritated by Clare's usual spoilsport reaction.

Clare, of course, knew, and she was correct, that whatever happened she would catch it for not having kept an eye on her little 'bro'. She had no intention of abandoning him this time.

"Well, what shall we play?" she said with as much enthusiasm as she could muster, believing naively that, by taking the initiative, she might control events a little. Uh oh. The collective eyes of the Owen children lit up like little sparklers.

"Hide and seek, hide and seek!" they chorused with enthusiasm.

"Okay, let's start with introductions," Clare suggested.

"We know you, you're Clare and you're great fun," they responded.

"Yeah, I bet,' she thought, "but not this time, brats."

"I know you know me,' she said gently, "but I can't remember all your names."

They all proceeded to introduce themselves anew. There was the eldest boy Harry; he was twelve, small and skinny for his age and as agile as a monkey and often found on the very top of anything which stayed still long enough for him to climb. Then there was Chloe who was a year behind Harry but, much to his irritation, taller and seemingly hitting puberty quicker than her elder brother was. Chloe had a twinkle in her eye and a misleadingly sweet smile that had been fixed at birth. These permanent features were the outward signs of untold mischief within and she was instigator supreme of the Owen posse. When it came to nefarious schemes, she would be the one with the idea and Harry, not wishing to be outdone, would pick it up like a baton, and run with enthusiasm.

Chloe's loyal lieutenant was nine-year-old Oscar. Oscar was round in face, round in limb and round in personality. He could charm the birds off the trees, or at least knock them off with stones, and followed Chloe's lead with the eagerness of a devoted fanatic. His bubbling personality was augmented by a rich and infectious laugh that was usually sparked off by the hatching of his sister's latest act of mischief. The two younger trainees were five and seven. Robert, the seven-year-old, was swiftly developing into a male version of his older sister, but with a little more ruthlessness and even better ideas. In fact, on occasion, she'd had to slap him down a bit, as she did all of her brothers from time to time, quite effortlessly. Whereas Chloe would convince some poor innocent younger cousin what fun it would be being buried up to their necks in sand, Robert would suggest doing it as the tide came in. Whereas Chloe recognised the need to consider some aspects of health and safety, Robert just didn't care. Robert had the face of a pixie and the personality of an orc but he lacked the guile and subtlety of his mentor. She knew how to operate to maximum effect without blowing her cover. She could achieve success whilst retaining an aura of complete and utter innocence.

Whilst Clare's prejudice was a phenomenon, based on experience, she nonetheless conceded that she had allowed herself to become paranoid when it came to the Owen children; they were, after all, only a bunch of kids. Except that was of course for Chloe. For all Clare's attempts to keep the children's playful exuberance in some degree of perspective, she struggled with the elder sister. Clare was convinced that, as a baby, Chloe had definitely been the victim of a kidnapping by some demonic woodland sprite and later released to become a disciple of evil. Her eyes, her simpering voice, her peevish smile, of all the brats she was the undisputed queen. Chloe was dangerous.

Thus armed with the memories of her previous encounter with the kids still raw in her mind, Clare reminded herself of the need to be vigilant. Clutching tightly hold of Jack she set off with Oscar who, whilst Chloe counted slowly to a hundred, led them to 'a really good hiding place'.

Making their way to the back of the barn, the three ran up some rickety stairs at and on to a dark and almost empty upper floor. Over in the corner of the huge space, just visible through the dust where a shaft of sunlight pierced the ancient roof, stood a large wardrobe, its door swinging invitingly open.

"Come on," said Oscar. "We'll all get in here."

Before she realised it, Clare had been ushered in with the door immediately shut behind her, allowing just enough time for Jack to be eased from her grasp. As she swung around in sudden panic, she heard the 'click!' of the lock.

"Oh no! I don't believe it," she cried.

"Oscar open this door, now! Oscar get back here, now! Oscar!"

But all she could hear was the sound of footsteps retreating back across the wooden floor accompanied by Oscar's manic laughter.

Neville, proud of his animal husbandry and vegetable self-sufficiency, was keen to organise a tour of his domain.

But before that, Bea had lead them to the veranda where she produced a bottle of locally distilled calvados, made from the previous year's communal apple crop.

"What's calvados?" enquired Gloria innocently.

"It's like an apple wine," said Denis nudging Eddie and winking.

"Oh sounds lovely," Gloria said, beginning to cheer. Things weren't perhaps so bad after all.

Along with the sugar cube to take the rough edge off the local brew, Gloria quickly downed the 'apple wine' and immediately began to be overtaken by a reassuring glow. After a second one, she declined the offer of the tour, preferring instead to remain sitting in the warmth of the late afternoon sunshine.

"You go ahead," she said, in a voice full of self-sacrifice. "I'll be fine."

Maisie, also keen to avoid a close inspection of Neville's turnips, offered to help Bea in the kitchen.

The boys set off with their proud host showing them firstly how the cesspit worked: how it could in part be recycled onto the burgeoning vegetable patch producing wonderful greens and how his next intended project was to harness the highly flammable methane gas that it produced to provide fuel for heating and lighting in the house.

"We used to do something like that at school," chuckled Eddie.

The two boys, already loosened up by the effects of the calvados, and much to Neville's irritation, broke into uncontrollable giggling. Leading them off towards his animals, he could only offer up grateful thanks that he had seen the light and escaped from the 'rat-race' before he too had been reduced to a gibbering idiot.

Realising that screaming was about as useful as if she were in outer space, Clare, still incarcerated in the wardrobe, had been rendered exhausted by flinging herself against the unshiftable door. She had by now reverted to trying to break out of the sides.

With one particularly determined effort, she managed to rock the wardrobe over to one side and on swinging back again it tipped right over and crashed to the floor. As it hit the deck, the door shot off, hinges and all. Scratched, bruised and very angry, Clare pulled herself up.

"Right!" she screamed. "Where are you, you brats!"

Back in the kitchen, Maisie was helping Bea prepare the vegetables for a meal. She had been impressed by the unusual size of the cabbages and intrigued by the strange, brownish colouring which all the outer skins of the vegetables seemed to share. Maisie was jerked out of her thoughts when Bea suddenly declared:

"I can't take much more of this, you know, Maise. It's doing my bleedin' 'ead in."

"Neville's become obsessed," she continued. "He thinks he's one of the pilgrim bloody fathers settling in the new world. All we need is an attack from a bunch of bleedin' Indians and he'd think he'd died and gone to heaven. You know, Maisie, I would love a long soak in a hot bath, my nails done and a night out on the town."

"Oh dear," said Maisie taken aback and feeling less than adequate to the sudden and dramatic outburst from Bea.

Putting her arms around her, Bea sobbed on her shoulder and then, after a few minutes, as if the whole thing had never had happened, she lifted her head.

"I'm all right now," she said wiping her eyes. "I'll be fine, I've got that off my chest, now is that fish soup ready?"

Having sensed that Neville was not amused by their juvenile behaviour, Denis and Eddie had managed to restore their equilibrium, and continued the tour trying to appear completely engrossed in his impressive flock of smelly, free range chickens and aggressive, spitting geese. Eddie even managed to control himself when Denis accidentally stood on a huge goose egg, which had lain hidden, for goodness knew how long, in a clump of dandelion leaves. Denis, fearful of irritating Neville further, tried to ignore the disgusting stream of putrid jelly that was running down his ankle and into his sock.

They were both much relieved when their host suggested that, as it was lambing time, they had better not go into the sheep pens but instead go back and see how the womenfolk were getting on preparing the meal.

"Womenfolk," thought Denis. "Weird."

When they got back to the veranda the calvados bottle was two-thirds empty and Gloria, having slid off the garden seat, was lying spread-eagled on the ground under the table. At that moment a red-eyed Bea followed by Maisie emerged from the kitchen at the same time as Clare, tightly holding onto Jack, came around the corner of the house followed by a grinning flock of kids.

"Oh my God, Gloria! Help me get her up, Denis."

Between them, the five adults managed to wedge Gloria into a chair and as she slumped across the table she moaned slightly which prompted Denis to contemplate asking her if she had enjoyed the 'apple wine' but he thought better of it.

The main living room of the cottage where they ate the meal was bare of any home comforts. An old-fashioned rug partially covered the slab floor and the walls were of bare stone. A small window on one wall provided minimal light during the day and a large farmhouse fireplace the heat. The table was a large oak one in the middle of the room, covered with a brightly designed blue oilcloth, with some kind of yellow and green flowers on it. The assembled multitude were seated around the table while Gloria, slowly returning from the land of the living dead, was slumped in her chair and slightly leaning against the wall. Clare, who was still seething, had been unfortunately placed opposite to her *bête noire* Chloe, who sat grinning across the table.

By the time Clare had caught up with the gang they had been just about to send Jack on his first space flight. Having bent down the branch of a particularly large tree and secured it to the ground with tent pegs and a piece of rope they had, using a second piece of rope, proceeded to strap to it a completely pliant Jack.

Wearing only an ill-fitting cycling helmet for protection, Jack was about to be launched into space by the cutting of the tether which was the only thing holding him on terra firma.

"I might have known," thought Jack, as spoilsport Clare suddenly appeared and set to screaming at his companions and generally ruining his fun as usual.

The kids disappeared in a flash and had only reappeared

again a few minutes earlier all around the table as if everything was just fine.

"Did you have a nice afternoon playing together, children?" enquired Bea.

"Oh yes, we had a great time," said Chloe, emphasising the 'we'.

Across the table, Clare realising the futility of saying anything, seethed. Chloe smiled sweetly.

The entire party, at least those still conscious, were relieved when, along with the piles of vegetables, Bea also produced a dish containing some kind of meat. They had feared that the bowl of fish soup, which only Eddie really relished and that was certainly not Denis's idea of French cuisine at its best, was going to be the closest they would get to meat.

"Oh this looks good, Bea," said Maisie, genuinely impressed. "What is it?"

Whatever it was, it was smothered in a thick deep red tomato sauce which smelt very inviting.

"It's *la langue de boeuf*," said Janet proudly.

"Oh lovely. *La langue de boeuf*," repeated Maisie, but she didn't have a clue what *la langue de boeuf* was.

Denis was still puzzling over the curious brown tinge which the all the vegetables seemed to share when Neville's tour, and the words 'cesspit', 'recycle' and 'vegetables' linked themselves together in his mind. At the same moment, Clare was scraping the tomato sauce off the top of the meat to reveal the taste buds on the surface of the 'cow's tongue' and Gloria, looking somewhat green around the gills, slid off her chair and onto the floor.

"Oh shit!" said Denis.

"Denis!" said Maisie.

"Oh yuk, I don't believe it, that's gross!" said Clare.

"Clare!" said Maisie.

And Gloria just went 'Barf' and vomited all over the floor.

"Mmm, lovely," said Eddie tucking in.

It was a fairly subdued procession that made its way carefully across the dark yard leading back to the car. As the Owens accompanied Denis and the crew there was the odd,

"Well it's been lovely to see you." And even a muffled,

"We must do it again some time."

But they all knew that, in truth, they existed at the opposite ends of a rather broad spectrum which had Gloria at one extreme and Neville at the other and that there were some rather major differences in lifestyle which meant that cohabitation, however brief, was probably not likely to occur again.

Maisie had a suspicion that she had not seen the last of Bea and that she would bump into her some time in the future in some town, on the town. Clare knew that she would never ever see Chloe again and as they shuffled along in the darkness, she carefully manoeuvred her foot to where she believed Chloe's would be and gently pressed down—BINGO!

"Oooow!!" screeched Chloe.

"Oh I am so sorry, Chloe, was that me?" said Clare in a simpering voice whilst at the same time swinging around and smacking her elbow into Chloe's face.

"Aaahh!!" screamed Chloe.

"It must 'ave been a beeg person oo stood on you," observed Doctor Henry, examining Chloe's broken foot the following day. "...and zat masseeve lump on your heyd! Ooh la la!"

Snuggled in the back of the car, making their way back to Monique's, Clare sat in the darkness with a grin on her face in keeping with one who had just exemplified the old adage, 'Vengeance is a dish best served cold.'

"I love you, Jack," said Clare giving her brother a huge squeeze.

"Ged off, you blimmin idiot."

Chapter Six

The decision to move on came after waking up for the second day to the sound of rain beating on the tent roof like tiny pebbles being hurled from some distance, and realising that the first thought after stepping out of bed was not where is the loo but where's there a jumper. The general consensus seemed to be that it was time to head further south. The theory was that once one had crossed the River Loire the weather would be much warmer. This was, in fact, generally the case.

It is one of the pleasant aspects of camping that packing up and moving on always brings with it a new sense of optimism and excitement, and so with renewed enthusiasm the team set about decamping. Even Clare joined in and it was not too long before what had been home for several days was tidily packed and had once again become the big rectangular box and secured to the car ready for wagons roll.

Before leaving, they made their way up to the house for breakfast with and to say *au revoir* to their hostess. Monique had been out early and brought back some lovely warm batons of French bread, which were quickly spread with chunky strawberry jam, local honey, or thick pungent lemon curd.

"Yummy, where did you get this gorgeous lemon curd from, Monique?" enquired Gloria.

"Sainsbury's, last time I was in England," she replied rather disappointingly.

Monique poured them out huge bowls of coffee or chocolate, which went down well while the men poured over the maps of Brittany and beyond. Along with barbecuing, map reading and route planning are more of those male preserves which men take very seriously and women let them get on with on the basis that is something far beyond their ken. It also gave the girls time to put on their faces, essential before setting off on a journey of any description.

It was not really rocket science to discover the best route to Nantes and beyond, it was just a question of getting out of Morgat and heading south, but the boys made the most of their role as leaders of the expedition. The only real source of debate was due to Eddie's desire to traverse the bridge, which he had found so impressive, one more time, and Denis wishing to take the more direct route down to Quimper. Denis managed to keep the argument going until he had taken the appropriate road off a roundabout so that any further argument was redundant, though it took Eddie several miles more before he realised. Once they had found their way past Quimper and on to the N12 they were on their way and, apart from the driver, they all made themselves cosy for the journey.

After several hours of uneventful travelling, it was time for a 'comfort break' and at the Aire de Bronzils they all piled out and headed off to find the toilets.

The Aire de Bronzils was an *aire* brimming with the kind of state-of-the-art facilities that are designed to perplex even those fluent French patrons who are able to read French instructions but for Maisie and Gloria it proved quite a challenge. In stark contrast to the prehistoric loos of the Perhidy campsite, the toilet of this particular *aire* consisted of a large silver cylinder, not dissimilar to the second to last bit of the Apollo space ships, the one that split in two and went hurtling off into oblivion. This particular NASA vehicle was already occupied when the two arrived for 'take-off', so they stood outside as patiently as is possible when one is desperate for a leak.

After what seemed like an age the door swung open and out of it emerged its previous occupant—three women!

"Good grief, these French!" thought Gloria. "Have they never heard of privacy?"

Perhaps it was the 'lost in space' theme that Gloria had subconsciously in her head, which explained why she approached the sliding door with some trepidation. It was, as it happened, with good reason, for no sooner had the previous astronauts stepped out than the whole thing burst into its post-mission cleaning routine, flushing every inch of its interior. Judging that it was safe to do so, Gloria finally stepped inside, as she did so the door slid rather quickly shut with a 'clunk!'. There followed a momentary lapse between the closure of the door and the illuminating of the cabinet, which, as a wave of panic overcame Gloria, had almost been long enough to render the toilet unnecessary.

Having established who was boss and elicited appropriate respect from Gloria, the space-age toilet settled down and after a while Gloria came out looking suitably refreshed and actually quite pleased with herself, another piece of

this quirky country conquered. Before Maisie had time
to react, Clare shot in next with Jack behind her. The
door shut as before, the light came on and Jack spotted
the hole in the ground.

"I'm not going in that!" he announced. "Let me out."

"You'll have to wait till I'm done, Jack, so shut up!"

Jack wasn't having any of it, he plunged his hand on
the big button on the wall and, as the door slid open, he
shot out.

"Stupid boy!" shouted Clare.

Sensing the departure of its occupant, the toilet
automatically slipped into cleaning mode. Jets of lightly
disinfected water shot out of walls, ceiling and floor. Clare
dashed forward just as the door slid shut and the light

extinguished. The last she heard was Maisie's scream. When the door reopened, dripping from head to foot, having endured a full body wash in diluted bog cleaner, a traumatised Clare was met with a small group of open-mouthed adults who weren't quite sure what best to say.

"Have you been?" enquired Denis.

"Denis!!" said Maisie.

Whilst the gals had been experiencing the delights of the state-of-the-art French toilets, Eddie had taken Maurice to get a cup of coffee. Never slow when it comes to embracing the most recent advances in technology, the motorway service station boasted the latest thing in fully automatic beverage dispensing machines. In a similar fashion to the technical toilets, the all-singing, all-dancing drinks dispenser could cause problems even to those speaking its language—with the added handicap of having to translate at the same time, getting a cup of hot coffee was no mean feat. Maurice managed to identify the amount in coins required to feed the machine, any combination amounting to one Euro, and Eddie, with the help of some imaginative miming, managed get the correct change from the Madame at the counter.

Maurice was immediately impatient at having to obtain a simple cup of coffee from a multi-dispensing vending machine but Eddie, a lover of all things technical, warmed to the task. Easing Maurice to one side so that he could concentrate fully on the instructions to the right of the business bit of the machine, Eddie set to his task.

His first attempt resulted in half a portion of what smelt like some sort of soup, which missed the badly placed cup and drained off through the grill underneath.

Undeterred, Eddie, having established that the machine had the capacity to provide just about any beverage one could imagine, identified that the one Granddad wanted was *café au lait, avec sucre*. The trick was avoiding the *aroma cocoa*, the, *café en grise, grand café sans lait*, the *cappuccino*, instant leaf tea, coffee without sugar, coffee flavoured with cocoa and especially the soups.

Unfortunately, the range of Eddie's vocabulary did not extend too far beyond *café*, so he had quite a challenge ahead of him. Having put in his money for the second go, Eddie at the last minute decided that his cup was still not quite in the correct position and attempted to push it up slightly just as the stream of very hot water began its descent down into the cup. Eddie had indeed been correct in his assessment about the positioning of the cup. Tragically, when the boiling water came down, though the cup was not in the right place his hand was. Muffling his true feelings to save embarrassment and barging Maurice out of way, Eddie shot into the washroom and plunged his glowing hand under the tap with the 'C' on the top, 'C' for cold of course...

"Aarrhh!!!" screamed Eddie.

With any thoughts of embarrassment being forgotten, he came running out of the washroom, waving his smitten hand in the air to cool it down. Very few of the occupants of the cafeteria bothered even to glance up to see what was going on, those who did shared with each other the usual Gallic shrug. They were well used to odd behaviour of *zee* tourists especially those of the Anglo-Saxon variety.

Eddie, now even more determined to conquer the coffee machine, which to him had taken on an identity and personality of its own, strode up to it threateningly.

"Right, café," he said out loud. "Right cup in correct place, money in, push button."

Down comes the coffee, down comes the milk.

"Bingo! There you go, Maurice," he said, turning to hand the coffee to Granddad but the space previously occupied by Maurice was now an empty one. Maurice, having lost patience long before, was sitting over by the window happily consuming the delicious cup of coffee he had purchased from the very nice lady at the counter.

By the time they re-grouped they were all, either suitably refreshed, or at least had had enough of their sojourn at the Aire de Bronzils, and were ready to continue their journey south. The clouds were indeed beginning to break as they began their approach to the crossing of the Loire. As they drove off from the *aire*, the girls in the back were very quiet after their close encounter with the French toilets and dwelling on what might have happened to them. Wedged between them was a bedraggled-looking Clare who had had to root through her suitcase to find some dry clothes after her very close encounter with the same French toilets and to whom the worst had actually happened.

In the front, as Denis turned right out of the car park, Eddie was causing untold confusion to the drivers behind, waving his injured hand out of the open window and apparently signalling left. Still, they were all safe now, and it wasn't long before their spirits picked up and conversations turned to what they were going to buy for tea after they had found the perfect campsite. Unfortunately, as is usually the case with these journeys, progress seems to be swift at the beginning and then begins to drag. Consequently by the time the terracotta roof tiles signalling their arrival south of the Loire began to appear, Denis was driving with the more usual accompaniment of the big zzzzs.

When the occupants of the back of the people carrier began to stir, they were surprised to see that the sun was setting and it was getting dusky.

They had travelled a considerable distance south of the Loire and were somewhere east of La Rochelle. It looked as if the evening meal of steaks and fresh fish off the barbie, drooled over in the earlier conversation, would have to be put on hold for the time being anyway, and they would have to make do with whatever they had in the provisions box, beans probably. They would also have to find a campsite before too long, otherwise they would be searching in the dark. They had been there before and it was not an experience they would wish to repeat.

Shortly afterwards, they came across a sign which read *Camping à la Ferme*, with a nice clear arrow pointing in the direction of the next left. Denis, taking full advantage of the slumbering women in the back, made an executive decision and headed off down the little country road and in the direction of the farm site. In the mind of Denis, he was heading for rural idyll, a babbling brook and quiet meadows full of buttercups being gently munched on by friendly dairy cows. The following day these same cows would submit their lovingly produced, full-cream milk to the farmer who would arrive, skipping down between the tents, bringing it by the brimming jugful to the happy campers. They would waste no time in pouring the icy cool ambrosia onto their crispy corn flakes, which Denis wasn't sure if they had in the provisions box, but oh, what the heck! Before he had managed to resolve this minor problem, a voice from the back brought him back to reality:

"Where are we, Denis?"

"Where are we? Good question, Maisie," Denis replied cagily.

Knowing Maisie's aversion for farm camping and with the visit to the Owens still fairly fresh in their minds, Denis knew that he would have to handle this carefully. There was also Gloria to win over, though, to be fair, she hadn't too much recollection of her last visit to a farm and anyway that was Eddie's problem, he thought, without much conviction.

"Well we have left the main drag south and I, er, we have been really lucky that me and Eddie have managed to spot a sign for a rural campsite that we are now heading for. Isn't that right, Eddie?"

Eddie, restless since purchasing his polycarbonate fishing rod in Quimper had, since seeing the sign for the farm campsite, been knee-deep in Denis's babbling brook and landing rainbow trout by the score, and was therefore right with him.

"That's exactly right, Denis, a rural campsite is in our grasp."

Just as another low-hanging branch hit the windscreen and the front wheel of the car hit another rut in the road which had by now become a bit of a cart track, Maisie declared, "Okay, Laurel and Hardy, quit the crap. We're going on a farm site, aren't we, Denis?"

"Yes dear. It's getting late, it's getting dark, we have found a campsite, it's only for one night. Any better ideas?"

"One night! Too right it is! Gloria, wake up. We're going on a farm site."

"Oh Gawd," thought Eddie, as his wife stirred.

"Oh dear," thought Denis as they arrived at the field, which was the farm site.

There was no sweeping meadow with waves of golden buttercups swaying in the breeze, the cows were sheep and even the babbling brook more of a dried-up quagmire at the bottom of the field.

"Never mind," thought Denis. ever the optimist.

He was further buoyed up when the little man, who came out to greet them, though bereft of even a smattering of English, was so obviously delighted to see them—and they did have the choice of any pitch on the field. In fact, as he pointed out, waving his arm expansively, the whole field.

Monsieur Ghrimas, bronzed and wrinkled from his sixty years in the open air and complete with a blue beret and a cigarette hanging from the corner of his mouth, wasted no time in taking their details and showing them the ablutions which were, if a little basic, very clean.

After showing them each of the facilities, the sink, the toilet, the shower, the water taps he would ask reassuringly, "Tres bien? Oui?"

He was even able to offer milk, bread, and duck eggs, so things, it seemed, were not quite as bad as the girls had feared and it was only for one night.

After managing to find a relatively level piece of field, Eddie wasted no time in setting up ready for the assembling of the tent whilst Denis got things ready for tea and Gloria went off for a shower. Clare and Jack went exploring and Maurice continued his snooze in the car.

"Exposure of the zip," instructed Eddie.

"Exposure complete," confirmed Maisie, his loyal assistant, though certainly not the apprentice in the operation.

"Coupling of the connectives, followed by connection of the poles."

"Connection complete, Eddie."

'Semi-erection of south poles, proceed to north pole, watch out for polar bears." This always made Eddie chuckle.

"I'm at the north pole, Eddie."

"Continue with semi-erection of both poles."

"Semi-erection completed."

"Prepare for enrobing of the frame. Watch out for protection of the prongs."

"Enrobing completed."

"Prepare for raising of the frame."

"In position, ready to proceed."

"Go, go, go."

"Election."

"Check."

"Selection."

"Check."

"Connection."

"Check."

"Erection."

"Check."

"Right, initiate docking procedure."

"Docking complete, go straight to pegging down."

"Need any help?" enquired Denis.

Maisie just smiled sweetly.

"Tea had better be good!" she said, as she smashed

the mallet down on the head of the last tent peg securing the whole thing in place. Eddie was as usual well pleased.

Tea wasn't bad: it was amazing what you could do with some garlic and onions, a few tomatoes, a tin or two of meat and various herbs and spices. Gloria had enjoyed her shower, which was cut short when a pair of antennae suddenly appeared from behind a loose wall tile, but even so she was quite content. Maisie too felt better after a nice warm shower and was beginning to be seduced by the peacefulness of the scene. That was until, while walking back to the tent in the dark, she happened upon something soft and slimy under her foot, which oozed into her toeless sandal, causing her return to the washrooms to clean off the sheep dropping. When she finally got back to the tent, Denis was sitting outside staring up into the starry sky.

"Castor and Pollux, Maisie."

"Yeh Denis, Castor and Pollux to you."

"One night, Denis, one night," she repeated as she squashed her third mosquito.

Chapter Seven

When Eddie awoke the next day he had just one thought in his head: "Fishing!"

Denis, never an enthusiastic fisherman, was, unusually for him, not the first awake and was still very much enjoying his slumbers when the sound of Eddie's stage whispers first broke through the canvas and into his subconscious sleeping head. The sounds of 'Denis, Denis', rather than stirring him into life were immediately given a lead role in his current dream.

Denis, resplendent in his bearskin cloak and knee-length leather breeches was leading a grateful party of followers amidst a huge flock of sheep into the safe haven of some distant planetary Nirvana.

Maisie and Gloria, bedecked in gossamer-thin silks, flowing freely in the vast expanse of space, were holding on to what appeared to be gently revolving miniature space probes and stared lovingly into the eyes of their redoubtable hero. Floating along at their side, holding hands and smiling sweetly at each other, were Clare and Jack. Maurice, accompanied by a retinue of female groupies, sipped from a large double-handled vessel, held by two of his companions and, with Panama hat perched on his head, strode along contentedly.

The only thing to mar this otherwise idyllic scene was the irritating sound of 'Denis, Denis' coming from Eddie. Bandaged from head to foot, and positioned well at the back of the procession, he was struggling to keep up with the rest of the party and, forlornly, but with growing conviction and volume, was calling, "Denis, Denis, Denis!"

"Denis, quick, let's go off fishing while the gals are asleep, otherwise they'll want to up and leave," urged Eddie.

Denis, his dream coming to a sudden if premature conclusion, quickly cast off his bearskin, for even in his semi-conscious state he recognised the undoubted wisdom of Eddie's warning. He had said it was only for one night but at the same time he figured that once they were established and had enjoyed a good night's sleep he should, without too much difficulty, extend their stay at *Camping à la ferme* a tad longer.

"Okay, Eddie, I'll be right there, if I can get over Sleeping Beauty here without disturbing her."

Eddie, mission partly accomplished, retreated, tiptoeing quietly to the safety of his own canvas where he began to collect the range of equipment he needed for a day's fishing. Not being too sure whether it would be river fishing, or in a lake, or maybe even a big, mysterious pond, he decided that it would be wise to pack everything. It wasn't long before Denis appeared having managed to extricate himself quietly from the bed without disturbing Maisie.

The first thing they needed to establish was where the nearest fishing was. They were confident that Monsieur Ghrimas would be able to provide them with that information and so they set off to look for him. Before leaving they left a note pinned to the tent for Maisie and Gloria:

"Gone fishing, don't worry about tea!"

It may have sounded like enormous optimism, though in Eddie and Denis's case it was more likely massive delusion.

Monsieur Ghrimas duly obliged with the necessary information. They had a choice of tackling the fast-flowing waters of the River Vendee or *un grand étang* in which Monsieur Ghrimas reckoned lurked a mighty pike. The kind of distance involved in getting to the Vendee put the boys off a bit—they had spent enough of the previous day in the car—and the lure of the mighty pike was difficult to resist, though Eddie rather unnecessarily worried about how it would taste. Another major influence on their decision was their imagining the girls' reaction if they were to wake up to no car, discovering that, without a vehicle, they were stranded in a field for the day.

As well as directions to the 'big pond', Monsieur Ghrimas also kindly furnished them with a pair of wellie boots each. These proved to be a very necessary piece of equipment for their trek across the fields, which could be a little boggy, and more especially as they approached the pond. For a little man, Monsieur Ghrimas had disproportionately large feet so Eddie's boots were just about right, if a little tight. Unfortunately, for Denis, he had been given the boots belonging to the patron's son, which were rather too big for Denis, so as they began their journey, it was Denis's turn to trail behind. He was weighed down with the bulk of the fishing gear, which he dragged along, pulling his oversized boots through the ever-dampening grass. In a spooky reversal of his previous

108

night's dream, Eddie was striding along at the head, the leader of the expedition, his precious polycarbonate rod cradled lovingly in his arms.

"Eddie. Eddie," called Denis, forlornly. "Slow down, mate!"

By the time Maisie and Gloria had woken up, the sun was quite high in the sky. Clare had been up a while and discovered that the farm they were on had donkeys which could be hired for a day or part thereof, and she had already dragged Jack along to investigate further. Rather than feeling 'stitched up' by the disappearance of Denis and Eddie, the girls saw it as rather liberating. As Denis rightly foresaw, the night's sleep had made a big difference to their moods, the sun was shining and the bit about not worrying about tea on the note had been summarily dismissed. The first thought that sprung to mind was 'shopping'!

They soon had Clare and Jack organised with a donkey and a simple route map, provided by the affable Monsieur Ghrimas. It did occur to Maisie that the combined stubbornness of Jack and a donkey was possibly not an ideal combination. Add to this the infamous ingredient of Clare's legendary impatience and the possible outcomes just didn't bear thinking about. Still they both seemed to be happy at the moment, so it was probably best to make their escape while it lasted. They knew that they would have to buy food for tea but the rest of the day was theirs to explore the delights of La Rochelle, Niort or Fontenay.

"And after all this, heaven!!" they thought.

Because of a combination of problems Denis was experiencing with his boots, the rudimentary nature of the map provided by Monsieur Ghrimas and the good old phenomenon of the country mile, it took rather longer than anticipated before the intrepid fishermen reached the *grand étang*. The word 'pond' was actually a little bit misleading because the body of water at which they had arrived would have been better described as a decent-sized lake which, if it hadn't been for a recent lengthy drought would have been significantly bigger. The net result (no pun intended) of the receding of the waters was the presence of a ring of mud, about two metres in width, which looked deceptively solid and that Eddie and Denis had to negotiate before they could actually set up at the water's edge.

Denis's first tentative step onto the dirty grey border of the lake resulted in his right boot breaking through the thin crust of the hard-baked surface and sinking effortlessly deep into the quagmire. With his other foot on terra firma, he managed to extricate himself from the mud, unfortunately leaving his other boot behind.

"Bloody hell!"

Eddie didn't help Denis's annoyance by only seeing the funny side of his mate's predicament. Denis straddled the border of mud and relatively dry ground, with his sock hanging off his otherwise bare foot and dangling precariously over the greeny-brown slime.

"Nice one, Denis, nice one."

Realising that, if fishing were going to be viable, they would have to come up with some sort of strategy, Eddie wasted no time and went off in search of material for the construction of a platform to place near the water's edge, from which they could launch their assault.

Whilst he did that, Denis, after much struggling, managed to retrieve his boot from the rapidly enveloping mud and lay exhausted on the grass coated in the smelly stuff. It wasn't too long before Eddie reappeared, dragging what was left of an old rotten five-bar gate. "Perfect," said Eddie beaming. "I've got a good feeling about today." But then Eddie, in common with anglers the world over, always did have a good feeling about today; this didn't, however, prevent them from drowning millions of worms in pursuit of 'the big one'.

"I hope you didn't find that gate in a gap in a field," said Denis, who couldn't help smiling at his friend's unshakeable enthusiasm.

With the addition of a few leafy branches, kindly provided by a nearby tree, Eddie's platform was complete and dragged carefully into place as near to the water's edge as they could get it. It now only remained for Eddie to assemble his state-of-the-art equipment featuring his pride and joy, the polycarbonate rod.

Eddie had already pointed out to Denis numerous signs of life in the waters before him. Bubbles rising to the top were obviously coming from huge monsters lurking beneath and any kind of disturbance to the otherwise calm, still waters were undoubtedly being created by the huge fish lurking near the surface and just waiting to jump onto the hooks. Apart from the usual sticklebacks and the odd newt, the only thing Denis had ever caught had been a perch whilst trolling from a rowing boat on holiday in Ireland. Trolling with a simple spinner seemed to Denis a nice relaxed way of fishing, preferably from a slowly meandering boat but failing that he'd content himself with settling back onto their little jetty and launch out the occasional cast.

Like all good fisherman, Eddie, before assembling his *pièce de resistance*, set up his old faithful fibre glass rod with a simple float supporting a big fat juicy worm, which dangled tantalisingly for the benefit of any passing hungry fish which might happen across it. But that was merely the side show, the warm-up act to the star of the day, his polycarbonate special, which Eddie carefully began to adorn with all the equipment necessary to transform it from a mere seven-foot pole into the super-efficient fish catcher it was designed to be.

Eddie, having finally completed his elaborate preparations and having decided on the best combination of tackle and bait, the latter decision being somewhat restricted by the fact that the only bait that they had was worms, was about to launch his first 'pendulum swing'.

Caution and past experience suggested to Clare that taking on the responsibility for just one donkey as well as Jack was probably about as much as was sensible to manage, and three hours out on the trail an ample amount of time.

Monsieur Ghrimas had provided them with a rather old-looking beast with what seemed to be a fixed grin on its face, which Clare eyed ominously. However, despite its sinister smile, it did seem to be a very friendly old thing and cooperated completely whilst it was being saddled up and ready for off. Jack was beside himself with excitement and was already beginning to irritate Clare who was wondering whether she might come to regret this latest example of sibling bonding. Still it had to be better than visiting coffee shops with Mum and Gloria. "Yuck!"

As well a bag of oats for Peppi the donkey, Monsieur Ghrimas had also given them a simple route map leading them along a fairly well-worn trail which should be just long enough for the three hours they had hired the donkey for. By the time they had gone through the gate and into the first field, Jack, perched on top of the donkey, was already becoming a bit frustrated at the speed at which they were progressing. Even worse, when he dug his heels into Peppi's side and shouted, "Yah!" it didn't seem to make any difference. To Clare, who had already issued the warning about how if he didn't pack it in, he would be walking, the coffee shops of La Rochelle were beginning to seem more attractive by the minute.

"A 'pendulum swing'," explained Eddie to a fascinated Denis, "is an elaborate way of casting, which as its name suggests, involves swinging the loaded line in the manner of a pendulum, though not simply too and fro, but rather more in the shape of a figure of eight. The trick is to time the actual moment of casting to coincide with its optimum position, so as to get it as far into the sea, or lake, or river as possible, because that, as everyone knows, is where the big beasts are."

As Eddie explained this to Denis, he simultaneously demonstrated the technique, swinging the line around his head and at the crucial moment letting go. Eddie's first cast wrapped itself around the branches of the tree that had so generously provided them with the covering for their jetty. In an act of seemingly cruel vengeance, the tree had conspired to wave one of its remaining lower branches into the path of Eddie's fishing line which had been winging its way to the middle of the lake.

"Damn it!" said Eddie.

"Yeh. I think I've got that, Eddie," chuckled Denis.

After a few cautious pulls, Eddie conceded that the only way he was going to release his line was by climbing the tree.

"This should be fun," thought Denis.

If Eddie thought at that moment that things could not get much more frustrating, they did.

Denis, having nonchalantly sent out his latest cast felt a pull on his line and, reeling it in without too much difficulty, found that he had secured a decent-sized rainbow trout, just big enough for a smallish pan but well worth cooking.

"Right!" thought Eddie, as he began clambering up the tree.

Clare's map led them across several fields and into pine forest where they stopped to eat the bread and cheese, which Clare had sensibly thought to pack. Jack at first complained that he wasn't eating it because the bread was too hard but soon relented when Clare said, "Fine, Jack, don't have anything then. I'll give it to Peppi."

After they had eaten, Jack gathered up a whole collection of pine cones and managed to cover himself in sticky resin but still he was happy. Clare, despite her initial misgivings, was actually enjoying herself. Peppi had been fairly compliant, the sun was shining and Jack, after having come to terms with the reality of riding on a donkey, was behaving himself. The next part of the journey was to take them around a big pond.

The lower branches, which Eddie had previously relieved the tree of to complete his jetty, would have come in very handy just now as he struggled to get off the ground. Eventually, having managed finally to get a foothold on the tree, Eddie swung himself up into the lower branches and, perching precariously astride a thickish bow, he peered down through the tree trying to see where his tackle was. By the time he had arrived at this point Denis had infuriatingly landed another pan-sized rainbow trout and shouted at Eddie to hurry up before he emptied the lake. It soon became evident to Eddie that there was no possibility that the branch at the end of which his line was tangled would in any way hold his weight.

"Denis," Eddie shouted, "Denis, if I climb to the end of this branch so it dangles down, can you get to the end of it and see if you can release my gear?"

"Yeh, but the end of your rod is twitching like crazy. Just let me see to it."

"Just give it a tug," advised Eddie.

Denis managed to stand himself up and, picking up the rod, looked forward to landing another nice rainbow when, whoosh—the rod shot forward, and Denis came flying out of his oversized boots and straight into the lake. Clinging onto the end of Eddie's rod with all his strength, he went gliding over the water like a Canada goose coming into land. In his excitement Eddie lost his grip on the branch and started to roll off, just managing to grab a hold before he fell.

"Oh Gawd!"

As Clare came over the top of the brow in view of the lake she was immediately struck by a sight which, on the one hand, made her stop and stare but, on the other hand, did not really surprise her. Close to the water's edge were a pair of very large, unoccupied Wellington boots, whilst, floating about ten metres from the shore, she could see a head which she immediately recognised as her dad's, one minute bobbing up and down in the water and the next, shooting off once again across the lake, accompanied by a "whoah!"

Not far from the shore was a huge tree and hanging from its lowest branch like the parachutist of St Mere

Eglise, was another figure, also shouting, 'Whoah! whom she immediately recognised as Eddie.

"Oh look, Jack," she said quite matter-of-factly to her little brother. "There's Dad and Eddie fishing."

"Wow, can we go fishing, Clare?" he replied, not really registering that there was anything unusual about the scene down by the lake.

"Let's go down and see," she said.

Eddie, feeling that he was too high up to jump was, with his scalded hand throbbing, struggling to continue holding onto the branch. Though having, as yet, no idea as to how she might help, he was still hugely relieved when Clare appeared along with Jack and a donkey. Clare being naturally more concerned about her dad, who was about to begin his second circuit of the lake, suggested to Eddie that he wasn't anywhere nearly as high as what it probably felt like and that he should just jump.

"Yeh, jump! Jump!" shouted Jack encouraging him. This was turning into a fun day.

"Look," she said, "I'll bring the donkey underneath you and you can try and land on his back."

Eddie wasn't sure about the wisdom of this and Peppi, no dumb ass himself, wasn't having any of it. By the time Clare had dragged the struggling Jack off the donkey's back and managed to manoeuvre it underneath him, Eddie's grasp finally quit and as he came down, Peppi did a little shuffle, and Eddie missed him by quite some distance.

"Oh Gawd!" he cried. "I've broken both me ankles."

"Are you all right, Dad?" called Clare from as near to the shore as she could safely get.

Denis had long since abandoned any romantic notions of returning triumphantly into camp with the mother of all pike or whatever this monster was. He had also had enough of the assisted swimming trips around the lake and, every time the fish stopped, his wet clothes were causing him to sink deeper into the water.

"Don't let go!" shouted Eddie, who was sitting up now and having been rescued from his own predicament could fully concentrate on his mate. Clambering to the edge of the makeshift jetty, he was urging Denis not to give in.

"Try getting into the shore," he called helpfully.

"Oh good idea, Eddie, I never thought of that one."

Denis, despite his exhaustion, was making some progress towards the edge of the lake when the line he was desperately holding onto suddenly went slack and the ripples on top of the water some distance away started to move in his direction.

"Bloody hell!" thought Denis as the adrenaline rush propelled him shoreward. He didn't know much about fish but he knew enough to know that pike had teeth and the bigger the pike, the bigger the bite. He couldn't remember at which point he had finally let go of the rod, he just remembered slithering out of the lake through the thick slimy mud and collapsing exhausted on to the grass.

"You all right, Dad?" enquired a concerned Clare.

"Where's the fish?" said Jack.

Eddie, obviously relieved that Denis was out of the water and safe, was managing to hide his disappointment well. He had already, in his mind's eye an image of himself showing around the photograph of the huge pike, which he and his mate Denis had caught whilst on holiday in France—all those mockers and doubters silent with admiration—but it wasn't to be.

"Never mind," said Denis, as he recovered his breath, "We've still got the pan-sized rainbows to show off to Maisie and Gloria. They can cook them for our tea. Now where did I leave them?"

Glancing over to the place where Denis had left his precious catch, they were just in time to see the last bit of the tail of number three disappearing into Peppi's mouth.

"Oh no!" gasped Eddie. "Donkeys don't eat fish!"

"Bloody French ones obviously do," said Denis.

"I hope the gals ignored our note and have bought something nice for tea," said Eddie as they trudged back. "I'm starving."

Eddie struggled on his aching ankles while with every step Denis's movements became increasingly less fluid as the smelly mud covering him from head to foot slowly dried in the heat of the sun.

Clare having discovered that Peppi enjoyed nothing better than a nice after-dinner mint, was coaxing him along by throwing the mint imperials, she had brought for him onto the trail as far as he could see ahead of him. He fairly galloped up to each one and then did not stop until he had finished munching, at which point Clare just simply threw another one. Jack thought this was great and every time Peppi shot forward let out a great, "Yahooo!"

By the time Eddie and Denis arrived back at camp, Maisie and Gloria had been given a graphic account of their fishing exploits by Clare and were sensitive enough not to rib them too much. Fortunately, there had been not the slightest chance of them taking too literally the bit on the note about tea so they had managed to pay a visit to the hypermarket on the way back from their shopping expedition and produced some nice red wine to cheer the boys up.

"We're just waiting for you men to get the barbecue going," said Maisie kindly trying to encourage illusions of adequacy in the minds of their pathetic looking husbands.

"All I want is a shower," sighed Denis, turning to go off to the ablutions.

"You'll be lucky, Denis. The waters been off since we got back from town."

"Bloody hell," replied Denis, looking like the monster from the deep lagoon.

After drinking the best part of a bottle of wine accompanied by the usual beers and digestives, Denis and Eddie were feeling much better. Gloria and Maisie did feel genuine sympathy for their sad partners and, as the sun went down on another day under canvas, gently stroked their wounded egos. It only then occurred to Eddie to ask where Maurice was.

"He's sleeping at the farmhouse apparently," said Gloria.

"Yeh, he got talking to Monsieur Ghrima's wife, who actually turned out to be his sister, if you see what I mean. She apparently said that a gentleman of his age shouldn't be expected to sleep in a tent and that she would find him a nice cosy bed in the house."

"Cor, what a guy," smiled Denis, his face literally cracking.

There had been no further talk about rushing off to find a proper campsite from the girls; after all, they had only barely covered La Rochelle—the shops of Niort and Fotenay were still eagerly awaiting their arrival.

Jack had had a great day and fell asleep shortly after tea, dreaming of cowboys and donkeys. Even Clare had had a good day. On reflection she felt that she had coped very well with a situation with the potentially disastrous mix of her brother Jack and a donkey. One way or another, she had got the better of both of them, no mean feat.

Unfortunately for Dirty Den the water still wasn't on when it was time for bed and, despite Maisie's genuine sympathy for him, it didn't run quite that deep.

"I'm sorry, Denis, but you are not getting into bed stinking like that," she told him, in no uncertain terms. "You'll have to sleep outside."

Curled up on a half-blown-up lilo, Denis lay in the open air beginning to have heretical thoughts about *camping á la ferme*.

It didn't help when Maisie enquired mischievously, "How are the stars looking tonight, Denis?"

"Pollux," he muttered, quietly under his breath.

Halfway through the night, Maisie's heart melted and, leaning out of the tent, she threw him another blanket.

Chapter Eight

By the time the sun began to rise on the next day Denis was covered from head to foot in a thin layer of silvery dew. His restless night had been punctuated by dreams, generally involving icy cold water, that were so close to consciousness they kept waking him up.

The blanket, which Maisie had kindly provided him with, had at least managed to prevent him from getting hypothermia. But, even on the right side of the Loire, lying under a cloudless sky at night on the damp grass, with the last of the air escaping from his lilo, this had been no happy experience. The only advantage was that when the water came back on in the middle of the night Denis was in pole position to take advantage of it and, after managing to de-ice his frozen limbs enough, he struggled his way up to the washrooms.

It wasn't exactly a hot shower but at least it was far warmer than the ground on which he had spent the night and he made the most of it.

When he got back to the tent, the sun was beginning to climb and the signs were that it was going to be another hot one. There wasn't much chance of anyone else getting up just yet, except for Jack who was disappearing to relieve himself behind the tent, as Denis was on his way back.

Feeling quite awake after his trip to the washroom, he decided that he wouldn't bother disturbing Maisie, so he made himself comfortable on a camping chair and promptly fell asleep. By the time the others began to stir, it was turning into one of those days when the tents quickly become oppressively hot and, one by one, the aroma of Eddie's pot of coffee succeeded in drawing them out.

With his head lolling on one side and his mouth wide open, Denis looked quite comical slumped in his camping chair. Jack, still half asleep himself, was tempted to wake him up by sticking a piece of grass up his nose but he couldn't find a blade long enough so he just curled up on his mother's knee and chewed on a piece of baguette.

"He looks comfortable on that chair," remarked Gloria, observing Denis. "It's obviously not as bad sleeping in the outdoors as you would imagine."

"Yeh, I thought he would have been quite cold but he looks ever so comfortable. He hasn't even bothered to use the blanket I sacrificed for him, ungrateful git! Mind you he looks remarkably clean now; I wonder if he still stinks." This last remark had them all giggling.

Denis gave a huge sigh as if he were waking up but didn't. In fact, he didn't wake up until the early afternoon by which time the girls had disappeared off into town, courtesy of Monsieur Ghrima and his truck. Eddie was sitting in the shade of a tree auditing his fishing equipment and coming to terms with the loss of his old faithful fishing pole and ten pounds' worth of a 'Rapala Skitterpop' fishing plug which was left behind when he had rescued his new rod from the tree. Still he hadn't lost his treasured polycarbonate rod, and there would be other days, better days.

He was even more cheered up when Denis suggested that they went and got some fresh fish to barbecue for tea to make up for the previous night, and off they went.

Denis knew exactly what he had in mind. From the first time he had seen them in huge pans in the local shops he had always wanted to make a paella. This idea was greeted with equal enthusiasm by Eddie who suggested that they went their separate ways and by way of competition produced a paella each, and see which one turned out to be the best.

Setting off back towards Morgat, they stopped at the first available hypermarket and the contest began.

A bit of competition always provided inspiration and Denis knowing that the main ingredients of the dish were fish and chicken was determined to embellish this a little and produce a 'paella extraordinaire'. He wasn't going just to have your basic fish in his paella, he'd have mussels as well as *crevettes rouge*, and a couple of langoustines for decoration.

Eddie's thinking was far more simple but clever and the first thing he did after getting his trolley was to go straight to the shelves containing the glass jars in which the ingenious French preserve everything from simple vegetables to *Confit de Canard* and the more exotic *Poulet aux Ecrevisses, sauce a l'Armagnac*. Somewhere in the middle of this impressive collection was just what Eddie was looking for—a nice big jar of paella. He wasn't going to buy one and pretend that he had made it, but simply look at the ingredients to ensure that his creation was as authentic as possible. What he hadn't considered was that the ingredients on the side of the jar were in French and here he struggled a bit. But Eddie at least also knew that the main ingredients were chicken, prawns, and of course rice.

Armed with this knowledge and with the help of the illustration on the jar, Eddie was confident that he could manage to cobble together the rest of the dish. It also helped that by turning over the jar slowly in his hand he was able to identify certain other ingredients. He was just debating with himself whether the red bit was tomato or pepper when he noticed a young man in the store's livery staring at him curiously. When he finally asked him something in French Eddie replied, "No, I'm all right thanks, mate," and headed for the fish counter.

As he was directing his trolley in the direction of the unmistakable odour coming from the fish counter the only problem, the issue exercising his mind was, how did they make the rice yellow?

The fish counter presented such a selection of fish that Eddie's first reaction was one of minor panic but he felt better when he noticed the piles of variously sized prawns and bought a few of both the *crevettes rose* and the slightly bigger *crevettes rouge*. He did think of getting some other fish to put in but didn't really recognise any familiar types. Mussels he didn't even consider as he hadn't a clue how to cook them plus he had disturbing childhood memories of stories about people on holiday getting 'mussled' from consuming dodgy ones on Southend promenade.

He now only needed some nice pieces of tender chicken and that rice. The chicken was easy enough, a few pieces of juicy chicken breast and the rice didn't prove too difficult either because, amongst all the various types of rice on sale, he found a packet of *Parfum de Riz*. This was a simple box of sachets, which transformed ordinary rice into *riz à L'Espagnole*. The picture on the front of the box clearly indicating that *riz à L'Espagnole* was yellow!

Feeling very contented with his endeavours and the speed with which he had completed his task, Eddie set off to the checkout; he'd even remembered to weigh and price his vegetables and so was not anticipating any problems there. Having not had the chance to decide whether it had been peppers or tomatoes before being interrupted by the assistant, he had opted for both.

Getting through the checkout without a hitch was still a relief, giving him a lift that was reflected in the very chivalrous delivery of, "Merci Madmoiselle," causing the young girl on the checkout to grin broadly.

Making his way over to the side of the store, he awaited the arrival of Denis, whom he could actually see performing some kind of mime act at the fish counter.

Denis's ambitious plans were proving to be a little more troublesome to realise. He had a clear picture in his mind as to how the finished paella would look but as he went around procuring the various parts of the culinary jigsaw, it was beginning to become difficult to accommodate them in the ever-developing picture. As the langoustines vied with the mussels and the chicken legs for pole position on the top of the dish, Denis began to question his wisdom.

"Am I being a little bit too ambitious?" he thought in a fleeting moment of doubt. "Nah, it'll all fit in somewhere and, anyway, what could I possibly leave out?"

He'd got some nice pieces of chicken, legs and thighs and at the fish counter purchased some beautiful white Julienne fish which he would secrete amidst the rice which he knew he would need, He would also get some saffron to produce the characteristic yellow colouring. This proved more expensive than he had anticipated, and how much was he supposed to use? Never mind, he'd cross that bridge later.

Having acquired the bulk of the things in his picture, he went off to the wet fish counter to get the special additions to his paella, which would make all of the difference.

Like Eddie, he also wasn't sure how to cook mussels and it was this that he was trying to establish when Eddie spotted him gesticulating to the lady behind the encounter.

"You put them in a pan and how much water do you use?" he was trying to establish.

"Non, non," the lady was saying.

"You don't put them in a pan? Non casserole?" asked Denis, puzzled.

"Oui, oui, casserole."

Denis was getting rather confused.

"You put them in a pan, but you don't put them in a pan."

The bit about chucking out the ones already opened before cooking and then all those which remained unopen afterwards was completely lost on Denis. He was about to give up when the very nice customer to his right came to his rescue. He explained that you just put the mussels in a pan and heat them without water, being very careful to discard any that are unopened after a few minutes of cooking.

"Merci, merci, Monsieur," said the grateful Denis. "No water, how strange."

Finally, Denis was all set and ready for the checkout, which by now had all got lengthy queues at them. Halfway to the end of one, he suddenly realised that he had not weighed his vegetables but managed to gesticulate to Eddie. Unfortunately, Eddie was reluctant to leave his already paid-for trolley-load and pretended that he couldn't understand what he was on about so Denis had to rush back to the vegetable stall to get them priced.

When he got back some helpful customer had shoved his trolley to the back of the queue and he had to begin again.

By the time the two of them got into the car and were heading back, Denis was beginning to lose some of his enthusiasm for the contest. But he also knew that a couple of beers, back at the ranch, would soon see him right. Eddie, still basking in the satisfaction of his successful expedition, was quite excited about it and couldn't wait to get started.

"You just sit back and prepare yourselves for this gourmet delight," Denis announced to the girls, who themselves had only recently returned from their latest shopping adventure and were enjoying a nice aperitif.

"We are doing," replied Maisie.

"You won't believe what we're going to prepare for this evening's feast," declared Eddie.

"No, you're probably right there," thought Clare.

"Ooh, how exciting," said Gloria. "We're ready for something nice after our hard day around the shops of St Neort."

Having cooked his rice and coloured it with the saffron, which he thought he may have overdone a bit, Denis set about skinning and cooking his fillets of julienne.

"Want any help, Denis?" enquired Maisie genuinely, knowing that sometimes her husband's creations could take a while to reach fruition by which time the expectant diners were usually beginning to succumb to the effects of the pre-meal drinks.

"Nah I'm fine," he said confidently.

"You just sit back and prepare to be amazed."

"Oh really," said Maisie, winking at her friend. They both giggled.

"Yeh, you wait till you get your teeth into these beauties," chipped in Eddie, joining in with the build-up to the tea, and already well on with his creation.

Denis was now cooking the mussels but, still not convinced that the information that he had received was correct, was half-expecting them to start exploding around the campsite. They didn't of course and he was delighted when, having dumped them into the hot pan, they started opening up as if shouting, "What's going on?"

He duly got rid of the one or two that had failed to open, and, scraping them out of their shells, mixed several of the rest in with his rice. The chicken pieces he had bought were cooking on the gas burner but were taking rather a long time.

Eddie by this time had just about finished his paella and, much to his annoyance, was beginning to see what Denis was up to. Eddie's chicken breast had taken no time to cook and his rice looked perfect. He peeled a few of his prawns and cooked them in a little butter flavoured with garlic before mixing them in with the rest of the dish, tomatoes, peppers and onions. Finishing off the whole effect by decorating the top with the large unpeeled prawns, it looked very appetising and smelt even better.

"How much longer is this going to be, Denis? We're starving. Can we start on Eddie's?"

"No, wait, you've got to judge them. The best things in life are worth waiting for, Maisie," he said encouragingly, but at the same time anxiously turning over his chicken pieces which still didn't seem to be cooked through.

Eventually Denis's work of art was completed but, as he had imagined earlier, he did indeed have quite a problem in accommodating all his decorative ideas into the one dish, which he served up in a deep paella pan, especially purchased for effect.

Like a regiment of sentries, with their beady eyes still intact, and their long pink legs clinging on to the side, Denis had arranged his large prawns, staring coldly outwards from every angle. Behind these, as if in reserve, was a circle of the medium-sized prawns, placed in a more prone position and looking ready to rush forward. Between the two sets of infantry, which still in their shells resembled a series of beach defences, Denis had placed the rest of the mussels. Unfortunately, so that he could accommodate his chicken pieces, he had needed to squeeze the prawns and mussels together rather more than he would have wished. The effect was as if a serious skirmish had already taken place. In the middle of the chaos, and imperiously surveying the scene, sat an angry-looking langoustine.

The whole ensemble was rested on a sea of very golden rice, which was difficult to see underneath the noise on the surface.

The immediate general reaction was "Wow!" It certainly made Eddie's simple recipe look rather modest by comparison.

The two dishes sat side by side and there was little doubt about which looked the most impressive. Denis beamed smugly whilst the judges disturbed the surface of the dishes in order to taste the meals and to decide on the winner. The final judgement, however, was to be on taste rather than appearance and when the two were sampled the verdict was unanimous.

Despite it looking less like an evening meal and more like a work of art, in the opinion of the judges Denis's paella was far too fishy. Denis couldn't believe the crass ignorance of this judgement, it was, as he kept reminding them, an authentic paella with authentic ingredients.

"Anyway," remarked Gloria, "your rice is far too yellow, it looks like it's been painted."

"And yuck! You've got blood running out of the chicken," added Clare.

Denis, struggling to cope with the disloyalty of the last remark, looked to Maisie for support.

"I'm sorry, Denis," she said, "but it is awfully fishy."

"FISHY!!! It's meant to be fishy," he shouted. "It's a bloody paella!"

Eddie just smiled contentedly and didn't say a word. He really didn't need to.

There was far too much in both pans to be consumed in one sitting so Maisie decided to take what was left up to the farmhouse. It was actually the majority of Denis's that was left to make the ignominious journey and subsequently accepted with apparent gratitude by Monsieur Ghrima's sister. However, the final indignity for Denis was the sight of Monsieur Ghrima's cat running past the tent the next day with the once proud-looking langoustine hanging from its mouth!

Whilst delivering the paella Maisie had tried to catch a glimpse of Granddad but he was nowhere to be seen.

"Don't worry about him," said Gloria. "Knowing Dad he'll be just fine." This had been the first time Maurice had been mentioned by anyone since his disappearance. They had become well used to Maurice's wanderings and the old cry of "Granddad's out" had long since been replaced with "Oh look, Granddad's back."

The next morning, this apparent nonchalance about the fate of Granddad was about to change.

Chapter Nine

After a night, which had not gone too well for the girls, only serving to reinforce their prejudices about *camping à la ferme*, Maisie and Gloria had had enough of camping in a field and were determined to move on.

It had began badly when the electricity had gone off while they were at the ablutions, plunging the whole place into darkness. Jack had thought it great fun to head off with the one torch that they had with them and Clare managed to get back to the tents by chasing after him. The fact that she had a mouthful of toothpaste at the time didn't help her mood when she finally caught up with him. At the time the lights went out, Gloria had a face full of soap and couldn't find the towel, and Maisie had been on the throne.

Clinging onto each other in the pitch dark, they carefully negotiated their way out of the washrooms, but, after screaming vainly for Jack to come back with the torch, they managed only to disturb the slumbering sheep in the next field. This set off a cacophony of noise that seemed to involve every animal within a ten-mile radius.

Stumbling across the grass towards base camp, with only the eerie glow of the gas lamp shining through the distant canvas to guide them, they cut a pretty picture in the headlights of Monsieur Ghrima's truck when he pulled onto the track in front of the house.

"Oh zee Eengleesh, why do they drink so much? And such preety ladies too," he remarked to his son Victoire, sitting in the passenger seat next to him.

What had finally made up the girls' minds about moving on was a spot of donkey trouble—at about three in the morning, without warning, the donkeys who had never really settled from the previous piece of excitement suddenly started up with a hideous assortment of loud braying sounds. Commencing in one corner of the field, courtesy of one of the larger jacks, it soon had the others going and within seconds every jack and jenny around the campsite was competing to see who could make the most unpleasant racket. The first blast had both Maisie and Gloria shooting up in bed with fearful faces:

"What the hell is that, Eddie?" asked a terrified Gloria.

Next door, Maisie was expressing similar sentiments. Denis, barely awake, just grunted and muttered something about camels.

Eddie didn't even stir until he felt Gloria's elbow sink deep into his ribs.

"What's what?" he responded, unhelpfully.

"Right, that's it!" both girls muttered in unison.

And that is exactly the point at which they were at the next morning.

Having finally managed to crawl out of bed after their disturbed night, they were stretched out on their sun-loungers applying the day's first layer of war paint, as Denis called it, waiting for the men to get back from the washrooms. In the meantime, they were succeeding in increasing each other's levels of indignation to the point where, when Denis and Eddie got back, they had better watch out, their minds were well and truly made up and they were off, either to a really luxurious campsite or an hotel!

And that's when Victoire appeared and everything changed.

"And already in bed and snoring when we got back, oh it makes my blood..."

"Good moorning, ladeees. 'Ow are you today?" enquired the handsome figure towering over an open-mouthed Maisie and Gloria.

Dressed in khaki shorts frayed at the edges and a figure-hugging vest, the sight of the bronzed muscular Adonis addressing them left them in no doubt as to why Denis had found difficulty in filling his boots.

"Y—yes we are very good, er, thank you, tank you very much, yes," gabbled Maisie.

Gloria just stared.

"'Ow do you like a nice walk in zee dark after a plenty big drink?" he asked innocently.

"Oh th—thank you, that would be very nice," responded Maisie, struggling to get her words out.

Gloria just continued to stare, smitten.

"Good, I'm pleased zat you are okay. By ze way my name is Victoire."

"I'm M—Maisie."

"And I'm Gl...Gl..."

"She 's Gloria," said Maisie coming to her friend's aid.

As Victoire made his way back up the field, the two girls sat for a few moments in stunned silence before both simultaneously disappearing back into the tent. A few moments later they reappeared armed with the full range of their equipment and rushed up to the washrooms for some serious facial adjustments.

There was no further talk of moving on that day and, when Denis mentioned that Eddie had found a nice-sounding campsite at Montpon with a bar and a pool, the girls were strangely dismissive. Clare just sat very quietly keeping her thoughts to herself. She had been awake in the tent when Victoire had arrived and had overheard the strange conversation. She wasn't completely sure what he was on about and though she kept saying to herself, "I really don't believe this," she was secretly looking forward to the drama unfolding because she knew that, whatever happened, anything involving her mum and Gloria would be entertaining, and would inevitably all end in tears.

Unable to contain herself any longer, Gloria suddenly stood up after tea and announced that she was going up to the house to see how Granddad was.

Sensing betrayal, Maisie immediately responded: "I'll come with you—I could do with the walk."

The two figures with the spring in their step, striding up towards the house with their blouses adjusted for maximum frontage, were in stark contrast to the two that had stumbled back from the washrooms the night before but that was yesterday, pre-Victoire, and now they were on a mission.

Gloria still hadn't forgiven her companion for the disaster that had befallen her in the coffee shop in Quimper, for which, she insisted, Maisie was to blame and she was determined that 'zee walk in zee dark' was going to be her and Victoire alone. However, she was happy to have the support of her friend initially and she was confident that she would dispense with her later.

The farmhouse door swung open and, framed in all his glory, stood Victoire. Forgetting the reason for their visit, they both stood there momentarily speechless—not something which occurred very often.

"Ah, er—how's Granddad?"

"G—r—anddad?" repeated a puzzled Victoire.

"Maurice."

"Ah Maureece, come in, come in."

Maurice was seated at the table opposite his newfound friend Madame Delours, who was pampering to his every wish, and Maurice was loving it.

"Hello, what are you two doing here?" he asked abruptly.

"I think I probably know and it's not me you've come to gawp at."

Maisie and Gloria, taken a back a little by the last remark, recovered their composure as best they could. It didn't help though with Victoire in the room, occasionally brushing past them as he prepared to leave on some errand.

"We were worried about you, Dad. It's been three days," said Gloria.

"Yes, well, I'm fine, thank you. Have you met Victoire?" he added mischievously.

Like synchronised swimmers, they both blushed in perfect unison.

"I must go to prepare for my wark," announced Victoire, turning to leave.

"Wark? Work? Walk? What did he mean?" thought the girls: was he getting ready for the night walk that he had invited them on?

"Maybe he's going to prepare the cocktails," thought Gloria, getting ever so slightly carried away.

Standing there shirtless, in a pair of rather grubby overalls, Victoire was just as impressive as they had remembered him; in fact, the rugged look suited him even more. Unfortunately, it also rather suggested that he was more likely to be off doing some work rather than preparing for the 'walk' and when he picked up a mop and bucket on the way out this action seemed to confirm it.

"Ask him about the walk, Maisie!" urged Gloria. "Ask him, quickly, ask him!"

"You ask him!"

Catching the end of this, Victoire responded: "Yes, ladies, please ask me."

"Er, what about the walking at night?" offered Maisie bravely.

"Tonight?" added Gloria quickly, not wishing, her rival to gain the initiative too much.

Victoire, believing that Maisie was referring to 'work', proceeded to lead them careering straight up the garden path by innocently responding, "Oh yes, some time. But not tonight maybe, but as you say, zee weekend, yes maybe. Oo knows?"

This tantalising final remark, as he went out of the door, was all the gals needed to set their little hearts racing and their heavily mascara'ed eyelashes fluttering. The night walk with Victoire was still very much on the agenda.

Maurice and Madame Delours glanced at each other over the floral tablecloth, Delours with a knowing smile, Granddad with a knowing shrug of his eyebrows.

As the door closed behind him and the girls slowly

returned to planet earth, Gloria's thoughts turned to matters more mundane.

"Er, can I use your toilette please, madame?"

"Oui."

"Ooh, yes," replied Gloria, a little taken aback, adding, "Oh, er, yes thank you," with an embarrassed giggle, realising her confusion. Madame Delours showed her through to the loo.

"You two looked well last night," Granddad said to Maisie when Gloria had gone. "I don't know what you'd been drinking."

Whilst Maisie and Gloria had been negotiating their way across the field in the darkness of the previous evening, Maurice had been sitting on the veranda of the farmhouse, having a late-night *digestif* with Madame Delours, and had witnessed the whole scene.

"Goodness knows what Monsieur Ghrimas and Victoire must think of us English. I don't know who's worse—you or that daft Gloria."

Granddad's admonishment didn't make too much sense at first to Maisie so she hadn't said anything to Gloria. It was only later in the evening that mulling it over in her head it began to make sense and the colour drained from her cheeks.

"Where's Gloria?" she screamed, the panic rising in her voice.

"She went off dressed like a thirty-bob salad, about half an hour ago, said she was going to check on Granddad again."

Maisie sat frozen in a dilemma, suspecting that her mate Gloria, being unable to satisfy herself with the prospect of a shared walk at the weekend with hunky Victoire, had gone to take the initiative for herself. Gloria, she further realised, was still clueless that the two of them had completely and blindly misunderstood his remarks about 'night walks', 'night works' or pre-walk drinks. Her mind raced.

If she were to try to head her friend off by explaining the misunderstanding, she would probably not believe her. Anyway she'd been gone half an hour—goodness knows what mess she was already getting herself into; on top of which she had done her usual Gloria trick, trying to outsmart her best mate Maisie. It served her right really! But then, she couldn't leave her to her own devices. The longer Gloria was away, the more Maisie thought about it. And the more Maisie thought about it, the more she thought, supposing it was herself that had misunderstood what Granddad had meant? Supposing the whole pantomime about 'work', 'wark' and 'walk' had been a clever subterfuge. Supposing Gloria and Victoire were, even as she sat there, enjoying a woodland walk together!

"No," she concluded. "The sneaky cow! I cannot leave her to her own devices!" and off she stomped, up towards the house.

As she was approaching the pathway, the man himself, Victoire, came hurriedly running past from the direction of the shower, looking rather flustered. When he spotted Maisie he looked positively embarrassed and muttered, "Bonsoir, madame."

"Oh right, I see," thought Maisie, conveniently adopting the moral high ground. "That Gloria really is disgraceful!" and off she went, storming back in the direction of the tent.

In the meantime, Eddie had arrived back from the

shower, still wrapped up in his towel and looking a little bit anxious.

"You haven't seen Glo, have you, Eddie?" Denis enquired. "It's just that Maisie was getting a bit worried about her as she has been gone so long. She was supposed to be checking on Maurice."

"Nah," he said hurriedly, disappearing into the tent to get dressed. His return was swiftly followed by Maisie, looking even more agitated.

"Bloody hell," thought Denis, "this *camping à la ferme* is so relaxing."

By the time Victoire reached the house, there was Gloria hanging around the doorway.

"Bonsoir Victoire," she purred in a sultry voice.

This was the last thing he needed and he brusquely shoved past her in a very ungallant sort of a way, rushing into the house. Gloria, knocked back by this very blunt rebuttal, lost her balance on the edge of the step and fell into a rhododendron bush.

Just as Maisie was reaching boiling point, as she mulled over the events so far, Gloria came into view, returning from the house. Looking a little less 'glam' than when she had left, her expression suggested that this was not the best moment to challenge her, or to ask her how she had got on. In any case, she didn't provide the opportunity, as she too disappeared into the tent just as Eddie came out.

Fascinated, Clare had been sitting as a quiet observer, taking the whole thing in, and was now eagerly awaiting the denouement.

Sitting himself down with the others, around the dying embers of that evening's barbecue, he began to tell them that he had been in the shower with his eyes full of soap and that he had been conscious of someone else in there with him. Imagine his shock when whilst feeling around for his towel it had been placed in his outstretched hand.

"When I'd cleared my eyes," he continued, "there standing in front of the cubicle, staring at me strangely, was that Victor! I felt quite uncomfortable."

"Bloody hell!" grinned Denis.

"Oh my God," said Maisie.

The hideous scream, which simultaneously came from the inner tent, set the donkeys off on a manic round of braying putting all of their previous efforts, into the shade.

"I love you, Denis Wilson," Maisie said, giving her husband a big squeeze as they lay in their bed that night.

"Ged off," he laughed, pretending to push her away.

"I say—they're very quiet next door tonight."

The embarrassed expression on his wife's face was fortunately hidden by the darkness of the tent.

"You know, Eddie, as long as I live, I'll never understand 'em," said Denis next morning, as he helped his mate to deconstruct the tent.

"Bloody mystery they are. One minute dead keen to stay!" he exclaimed pulling out a particularly obstinate tent peg. "Next minute can't get away quick enough."

"Don't talk to me about them," responded Eddie, carefully folding down the inner tent.

"Gloria's up and down like the proverbial yoyo! She's been floatin' around for the last few days like camping in a field was what she was born to do; now suddenly she's got a face on her like a wet weekend and…'We're going today, Eddie, and I don't care where!' "

"Bloody women!" they concluded in unison.

By the time the ladies had emerged from their morning showers and face-painting session the bulk of the gear was down and packed.

Clare had enjoyed the last few days. Following the trails around the farm, she and Jack had ridden Peppi to exhaustion and would be quite sad to leave him. Peppi too had enjoyed their company, especially the mint imperials, but the characteristic grin on his face was particularly broad that morning when he noticed his erstwhile companions were getting ready to leave: now he could get back to his usual occupation of casually munching grass. There was a tinge of sadness all the same.

Apart from the main attraction of the donkey riding, Clare had relished the sideshow provided by her mum and Gloria. Though at first she had thought it all a bit sick, she had managed to overcome her prejudices as the action had picked up, reaching its exciting climax the previous evening. Like getting to the end of a good book, it all seemed a bit flat now so she was looking forward to moving on, especially to a bigger site with a swimming pool.

It was the promise of the swimming pool that convinced Jack that it was all right to move on. He had had a whale of a time living with the freedom of a huge field surrounded by insects, muddy swamps and wild animals (sheep and donkeys). He had been lost in a fantasy world of explorer, famous entomologist and wild west cowboy plus there was always Clare who, though generally a boring spoilsport preventing him from pursuing his more adventurous schemes, nevertheless had her uses when it came to steering donkeys.

The only real problem was prising Maurice from the clutches of Madame Delours but, like all true Casanovas, Maurice was an exponent of fickleness. Though he had enjoyed the company of his latest amour for the last few days, he too was ready to move on.

Even Denis, for whom rural camping promised so much, had mixed feelings about leaving. The memory of the freezing night he had suffered after the fishing trip was still fresh in his mind, and the humiliation of the paella competition would take an even longer time to expunge from his memory.

So as the people carrier made its way back up the track towards the main route south, they got a good send off, Monsieur Ghrima calling, "Bonjour, bon journée, bon voyage." Standing at his side, with a handkerchief to her tearful eye, was his sister, Madame Delours. In the field behind and sensing the excitement, Peppi was, with his head aloft, braying madly into the clear blue sky.

As they reached the end of the track there holding open the gate was the handsome, if somewhat sheepish, Victoire.

"Cheers, mate," said Denis.

"Au revoir, au revoir, Mesdames,'" responded Victoire enthusiastically.

"Seems a very nice guy," Denis added, winking at Eddie.

Just audible above the sound of the revving engine could be heard a muffed cry from the back.

"Women," thought Denis. "One minute they can't stand camping à la ferme, next thing they can't get enough of it."

Chapter Ten

"Right, Eddie!" said Denis. "Get the old map out, let's see where this Montpon place is."

It never took long for the mood to lighten and the enthusiasm to rise once they were heading off to pastures new and exciting. By the time it got to around noon-hour Gloria began to perk up. She had passed through the shame and guilt stages and her thoughts, along with everyone else's, had turned to food.

"Sanjohn dongelly," said Eddie. "That's where we're near for food. Sanjohn dongelly."

And there just to the east of the A10, on which they were heading south, was signposted the little market town of St Jean d'Angely.

After a quick look around the market which was just closing up for the day, giving them just enough time to buy some bacon for the next day's breakfast, they happened upon a little bar on the corner of the street.

From the outside it didn't looked much and inside there was enough room for not much more than the bar itself and several circular shelves built around thin pillars which in turn had several tall stools around them. What had attracted them in, as much as anything, was the chalk sign outside advertising 'Steak et Frites'.

"Sounds good," said Denis.

Nobody disagreed and they were not disappointed. Though, as they had learnt from experience, with only a limited grip of the French language, eating out in France could be a bit 'hit and miss', this was most definitely a hit. Each of them were served with a huge piece of entrecote steak with a choice of mushroom or blue cheese sauce, frites and a big salad, with a couple of ice-cold Stellas to wash it down—it was perfect. It was the kind of place that never seemed to have heard of anything as vulgar as profit margins but where Mr Patron appeared to gain as much pleasure from serving the food as they had in eating it.

Completely satisfied after the latest culinary success and after they had rescued Granddad, who had once again managed to lock himself in the toilet, they were on their way again and heading south towards Bordeaux.

It proved to be quite a bit further than they had realised and Denis hadn't helped by missing signs that would have avoided the odd town centre, though he blamed Eddie's lack of navigating skills. Whoever was to blame, it was getting quite late by the time they made their left turn and began their journey east. Having got over their little spat about navigation and seeing signs for Cognac, Bordeaux, Bergerac and latterly, St Emilion, the four of them could hardly contain their combined excitement— they were without doubt right in the middle of wine country. Combine with this the fact that the campsite to which they were heading had a river running alongside it, and Eddie couldn't wait.

By the time they reached Montpon it was getting quite dusky and after doing their usual trips down cul-de-sacs they finally spotted the sign 'Camping au Bord de la Rivière'. It seemed a long time since they had left the morning's campsite and they were all ready to hit the sack. It was rather too dark to get a clear impression of the site but there did seem to be a bit of life left in the bar and *salle de jeux*.

The town itself was festooned with garlands of coloured flowers strung across the streets, the petals having been made out of thin plastic sheets. The full magnificence and extent of this decoration, bedecking every avenue street large and small, was not apparent until daylight but even in the faint light of dusk it was still an impressive sight.

It did not take too long for Denis and Eddie to do the checking-in. The camp owner, who also obviously doubled as the barman, was a very friendly man who though not able to speak English was very patient while Denis carefully explained their numbers and requirements.

It was nice to see that there was still some life left in the entertainment facilities, which augured well for future evenings. For this particular one, however, they were just keen to set up camp and retire.

By the time Denis, tired after his long drive, was in bed and drifting off to the land of dreams, Eddie, having discovered a little hole in his foot pump, was still putting the finishing touches to their sleeping arrangements. As he fell asleep at the end of the first day in Montpon, Denis thought that he could hear the gentle sound of two alpine donkeys mating on the slopes of a mountain meadow— it was actually Eddie trying to blow up air beds till well after midnight. Hee haw, hee haw...*ZZZzzzzzz*...

When the sun rose on their new home the next morning it revealed, for the girls at least, everything which they could have wished for after the last few days in a farmer's field. Sitting on the edge of Montpon, the whole site was not overly large, which meant that nothing was too far away, and it was nice and flat. There were quite a few trees dotted around which, as well as providing shelter from the hot summer sun, gave the area a nice cosy feel. In the middle of the site stood an enormous toilet block—just a hop and a skip from their pitch—which contained individual cubicles for each toilet! Apart from these there were also other cubicles especially for ablutions and, more importantly for the girls, these included mirrors. As well as these there were several showers with unlimited hot water. As far as Maisie and Gloria were concerned, this was real camping. The only thing that left the girls a little bit puzzled was that they had found what were obviously the ladies' facilities but they couldn't see where the men's were.

Each pitch was bordered on three sides by low hedges which provided a sense of privacy and the grass was well groomed and clean—no having to avoid piles of unpleasant animal droppings whilst struggling up to the washrooms in the dark. There was even a water tap located just along from them.

While Denis and Eddie cooked the bacon, which they had bought in St Jean d'Angely the previous day, the girls made full use of the facilities and when they returned they were in high spirits. Arriving back at the same time as Clare and Jack, who had been exploring the games room and play areas, they all chattered happily, exchanging information. Clare and Jack were equally happy with their new surroundings and especially with the swimming pool. The fact that the River Isle wound its way around most of the site meant that Eddie was also looking forward to the next few days and the chance at last to register his first success with the new rod. There was a small bar adjoining a community room and a shop that sold various provisions, as well as the usual fresh bread and milk.

Located just the north of the famous Dordogne river, the area surrounding the campsite was very definitely wine-growing country inviting exploration and that is exactly what they intended to do but not today. After the long journey of the day before, today was a lazy post-travelling day, today was one for relaxation.

Gloria and Maisie, stretched out by the pool and covered in tanning cream, were, when they occasionally opened them, keeping an eye on Clare and Jack who, with the help of a large inflatable whale, had managed to accumulate quite a following of other young campers. This was an energetic bunch who joined in the game of launching sprays of water out of the pool and onto their respective parents or any other adults who happened to be lying at the side. After a while, Clare distanced herself from this group who were becoming rather raucous and whose targets were rapidly turning from being gently indignant adults into rather more irritated campers. Denis, who had been quite excited at the prospect of splashing around in the cool water, was disappointed to discover, from the evidence of the pictures on the wall, with big red crosses through them, that as well as 'eating', 'smoking', and 'urinating' in the pool, the other strict no-no was the wearing of shorts.

"It doesn't say anything about going in naked, Denis," said Maisie helpfully.

"And there's always your thong," added Gloria.

"Yeh, go on, Denis, give us a laugh," added Gloria. "Cor, look at those two over there."

It seemed from the evidence presented by the couple at the end of the pool that 'snogging' and 'heavy petting' were not on the list of outlawed activities. This didn't seem quite fair to Denis but he reckoned that the after the trauma he had suffered from exposing his buttocks around most of the Pink Granite Coast he had no intention of digging out those 'skimpies' again. So he mooched off into town to check out the tourist office and to see if he could find anything exciting for tea.

Maisie and Gloria, shocked by the antics of the young couple, suddenly started to take much more interest in Jack's safety and whilst they kept a careful eye on his activities in the pool they regularly reminded each other just how disgusting the other 'goings-on' were.

"It shouldn't be allowed, Maise," remarked Gloria having spied a particularly bonnie youth in a pair of the usual brief briefs.

"It should certainly not, it's outrageous! Glo! Just look at them now! Oh, I can hardly bear to watch."

By the time Denis got into town, the market was well and truly packed away and the shops were shut for the afternoon. So he went exploring up and down the various streets, admiring the magnificent decorations, which were resplendent in the sunshine. After wandering up and down the main street for a while, he did manage to find a small supermarket hidden up a side street which provided him with most of the things he needed and certainly, as you would expect, a fine selection of wine. The young girl in the shop greeted him in the usual friendly and respectful way, welcoming him and serving him as if he had been expected.

"Bonjour, Monsieur."

"Merci, Monsieur."

"Au revoir, Monsieur."

"Bon journee, Monsieur."

Denis then called into a friendly little bar and was once again greeted with a warm welcome. Ordering himself a *bière pression*, he sat outside in the warm sunshine, breathing in deeply and loving every minute of it. Having successfully conducted his whole mini-shopping expedition completely in French, he came away from the bar feeling very much at ease with Montpon and its townsfolk.

At the tourist office he discovered that the multi-coloured garlanding was the result of the combined efforts of the whole population of the town, who had spent the long dark winter months producing the flowers for decoration. Each town in the particular 'department' had taken its turn in hosting a festival to celebrate the rich and diverse trades of the region, and this had recently taken place. Denis smiled to himself as he imagined the town mayor going around the houses in January and February, checking up that, under the pain of death, they had completed their quota.

"Excellent," he thought. "You can't beat the French."

Significantly, what he also discovered was that there was a wine festival the next day in the nearby town of St Foy la Grande. He knew that when he got back with this bit of information it would be greeted with enthusiasm by the others, and he was not wrong on that score.

So with a spring in his step, and his love of France restored and represented by the baguettes sticking out from under his arm, he made his way back with the exciting news.

St Foy la Grande, about twenty kilometres directly south of Montpon and twenty kilometres west of the famous Bergerac, was decked out in bunting as befitted a town in the midst of its annual wine festival. Most of the streets had been cordoned off and laid out with a huge variety of market stalls offering a whole range of local cheeses, pates, sausages, meats, confectioneries, and, of course, wines. After the handing over a small fee for the purchase of a glass displaying the logo 'Syndicat Des Producteurs Sainte-Foy Bordeaux', the owner of said glass was then free to wander around all of the wine producers' tables and sample at leisure the wines which they had on offer. In an area overflowing with gallons of wine, this was like handing out free water. The purpose of this exercise was to ascertain which wine they wished to acquire for their hotel, restaurant or simply for domestic use. This was an arrangement that was obviously open to abuse by unscrupulous visitors to the festival who may choose to buy the glass at the nominal cost and then spend the day enthusiastically imbibing the delights of the region with no intention of making a purchase, but simply to get sloshed. Heaven forfend that this was the rationale that was in any way in the minds of Denis and his party; it certainly had never occurred to Jack, though it hadn't taken Clare too long to cotton on.

As it happened, there were too many distractions amongst the wonderful variety of stalls to confine even the most ardent philistine to such a narrow agenda. Before they had got remotely close to the 'fruit of the vine', Maisie and Gloria were stuck amongst the cheese and pates and it wasn't long before the group was fragmenting—each distracted by the various sights and sounds around them.

Denis and Eddie stayed together for a while and were watching a group of young men competing with each other in rolling oak wine casks down a marked-out course on the cobbled street to establish who had the most testosterone. It was no use simply trying to roll them as the bow shape sent them off in all directions, the technique was more of a continuous toss-tail-over motion. This was quite a demanding task, and the bare-chested men involved sweated profusely as they heaved the heavy objects over and over towards the finish line. One particular red-faced competitor, who had obviously spent some time at the wine sampling before finding his way to the cask racing, was struggling even more than the others and looked as if he might pass out.

"I wonder if that cask is a barrel or a firkin?" remarked Denis casually.

"I wouldn't know," replied Eddie, "but he's certainly taking his firkin time with it."

The peals of laughter that greeted this juvenile witticism were mistaken by the struggling competitor as howls of derision and he turned the glare of his bulging eyes in the direction of the mirth. The boys had also unwittingly attracted the attention of the extremely large cooper who was organising the event. Wearing a huge leather apron and with hands like spades, he immediately identified two competitors for the next heat in the competition and began striding towards them. Sensing that in this situation discretion was the better part of valour, our heroes felt that the time had come for them to slip off discreetly into the crowd and make good their separate escapes. Eddie soon stumbled upon the fish counters, which kept him distracted for a while.

Clare and Jack had joined a troupe of dancers in bright costumes who were doing some sort of conga around the square. Actually, Clare had become a rather reluctant member of the troupe when Jack had gate-crashed one of the dances and refused to move on.

"Jack, come here, you idiot," she called in vain.

"They're a proper group, it's not for anyone to join in."

After several attempts to dislodge him with an assortment of threats and entreaties Clare resorted to, "Jack, now!"

This latest, more threatening command, was lost in the bedlam of pipes and drums, and only resulted in Jack, who was skipping around after the dancer at the end of the line, leaving his imaginary tin whistle to thumb his nose and wiggle his fingers at his boring sister. To his boring sister's deep embarrassment, this brought appreciative laughter from several of the spectators and one or two of them, following Jack's example, joined in the dancing too. Clare, confident in the knowledge that when she got him back to the campsite she would kill the little brat, was too afraid of losing him in the crowd to leave him to it and had reluctantly joined in. The dancers seemed to be happy with the audience participation and before long the whole place was bouncing.

"Oh just try that cheese there with the black waxy shell," urged Gloria. "It's really yummy."

Maisie, herself in the middle of a generous piece of local

foie gras, was in no way slipping behind her companion when it came to sampling the delights before them.

"Mmm, have bit of this, Glo."

The result of the uninhibited sampling of the delights before them led them, whether intended or not, to make several purchases which they had decided would, as a change from the usual barbecue, make a nice evening meal for everybody. It also left them feeling a little thirsty and they knew exactly how that could be attended to.

Back in the square, the dancing was in full swing. Out of the crowd a little man whom Clare thought that she recognised, perhaps from the campsite, had joined in. With amazing muscle-bound legs and shorty-shorts he had his hands around Clare's waist as the whole crowd went swinging around following the band and the colourful dancers. Despite being press-ganged into it originally, Clare was really enjoying herself. Naturally, it was at this point that her contrary brother decided that he had had enough and decided to wander off, and reluctantly Clare had to follow.

Inevitably, everyone met up again around the tables displaying the reds, whites and rosés of the area and it did not take them long before they were making full use of their sampling glasses. Just beyond the last of the stalls was the intriguing site of several people, in groups of four, apparently sampling wine with blindfolds on. After watching for a while to see just what it was all about, it became clear that it was a wine-tasting competition. Denis did not take too much prompting by the others to offer himself as a competitor in the next round and the others soon followed.

The task before them was fairly straightforward. They

would be handed four glasses of wine one after another and they had to identify which was red, which dry white, which sweet white and which rosé; they let Denis go first. The group of people organising the event was thrilled to have some 'outsiders' join in the contest and perhaps anticipated some fun to emerge. Denis was blindfolded and the rules explained. It had been just as well that he had observed several rounds beforehand as the instructions were delivered in French and at speed.

The first glass was placed in Denis's hand and before taking in his first mouthful he carefully swirled it around in his hand put his nose to the top of the glass and expertly inhaled its bouquet. He then slowly took his first sip and allowed it to caress his taste buds gently before announcing with some certainty, "Rouge!"

He had known, almost straightaway, that it had been red but didn't want to make it look too easy.

"Bravo," confirmed the judge and tried to hand Denis the next glass. Denis, not being able to see this, continued to drain the first glass before taking the next one.

"Hmm," he thought. "This one is a little more tricky. Is it the rosé or the dry white?"

Another deep sniff before musing, "Dry means really dry, sharp dry. Tarty dry. This isn't quite that, it's quite mellow."

"Rosé," he suggested, with a little less confidence than previously.

"Bravo!" cried the man.

"Oh bravo!" chorused Maisie and Gloria proudly.

"Well done, Denis," said Eddie, genuinely impressed.

"This should be easy peasy now," thought Denis. "Only the two whites left. One sweet, one dry."

By this time Clare and Jack had arrived to see Denis blindfolded and drinking wine.

"Uh oh. What's he up to this time?" thought Clare.

It didn't take much time to identify the next one as being the dry white because he didn't much care for it, especially as it was a little bit warm from standing in the sun. The last one he made the most of spinning it around his mouth a few times before confirming its identity as the 'blanc doux'.

"Bravo, bravo," cried the man. "Bravo, Monsieur Anglais."

A round of applause followed from the little crowd that had gathered and the lady with the clipboard behind the table announced,

"Trois minutes et vingt-deux seconds."

"Three minutes, twenty-two seconds," repeated Denis. "Bloody hell, I was being timed!" he said disconsolately. "It was a bloody race!"

"Never mind, Denis," consoled Maisie. "You were great. Fancy knowing them all. Well done."

Eddie and Maisie were in the next group of four and both of them fell down on the rosé thinking it was the dry white but they were pleased with two out of four. Gloria then stepped up along side three French tasters, two men and a woman. She didn't approach it with too much confidence but, hey, she was going to enjoy the four glasses of wine.

"Allez," called the starter to the four competitors standing glass in hand, waiting for the signal.

No nonsense from Gloria. No sniffing, no hesitation. Gulp, straight down the hatch without touching the sides.

"Mmm nice, sweet white," she said. "Give me another."

Straight down.

"Easy, red. Next..."

"Yuck! Dry white."

"Rosé," she announced confidently before gulping the final one down. Looking around her fellow competitors were miles behind.

"Bravo! Bravo!"

"Une minute et huit seconds," announced the time-keeper. "Ze winner!"

It would have been nice for Gloria to stride up with pride to receive the acclaim of the crowd and be presented with four bottles of wine, a baseball cap and a pair of sunglasses. As it was, after downing the four glasses of wine on top of the others which she had been 'sampling' throughout the afternoon, she felt quite giddy and so it was more of a slight stagger than a gracious winner may have wished.

She, nonetheless, received her prizes accompanied by

the enthusiastic applause of the crowd that had gathered to celebrate the unlikely winner of the wine-tasting competition. Her companions, also sporting inebriated grins, clapped with even more vigour. Gloria, having out-timed a whole raft of locals, and, of course, Denis, was duly crowned Sainte Foy la Grand's latest 'Queen of the Vine'. Even Denis, who was still grumbling months later about not realising the competition had been against the clock, joined in the applause as happily as the rest.

The effect of their having thrown themselves unreservedly into the local culture was taking its toll and Denis was a tad worried about having to negotiate their way back to Montpon; he preferred to drive the car rather than to aim it. He needn't have worried.

As the sun was beginning to disappear behind the high buildings surrounding the main square, the spectators around the wine-tasting competition began to disperse to search out other attractions. The time had come to think about returning to the campsite and the evening meal, so where was Maurice? To be honest, Maurice had been left to his own devices after they had arrived in the town and had not really been seen after muttering something about needing the toilet and wandering off from the others. That had been a long time ago now and as it was nearing tea-time, this made Maurice's absence a little more relevant.

"Where is the old rascal? Has anybody seen him recently?" asked Denis.

Everybody looked down at the ground and shuffled their feet, a little embarrassed. It had seemed okay at the time to let Granddad wander off but it hadn't been too long ago that Granddad 'getting out' would have caused a panic and a search party would have been launched. Maurice, having recently more than illustrated his independence, had become more like a teenager than an octogenarian and it was proving just as difficult to keep track of his comings and goings. On this occasion, however, Maurice had wandered off in a strange town and he had been 'missing' for several hours. As the crowds began to thin out it was clear that he was no longer simply immersed into the general revelry.

"We saw him," Clare told them, "over there," pointing in the direction of a rapidly emptying space where earlier had been stalls with live animals.

"Yeh, he told me off for touching some mice. I only picked one of them up; it was smiling at me and squeaking, probably asking me to take it home and Granddad said, 'Put it down, it's dirty!' " said Jack, mimicking Granddad's angry voice. "But it wasn't, it was white and really clean and cute and..."

"Shut up, Jack," squawked Clare.

"You shut up, you pig!" he returned.

"Both of you now!" warned Maisie. "This is not funny."

"I wasn't laughing," muttered Clare.

"Well, we'll have to split up and go and search for him," suggested Eddie.

"He's probably in one of these houses here with some local wrinkly having a whale of a time."

"Eddie, that is not funny, but probably true," grimaced Gloria, half-heartedly slapping her husband across the head.

"He's probably sitting there watching us now," added Denis.

Sitting in the police cell, Maurice was neither accompanied by a local wrinkly, nor mischievously observing his companions' growing anxiety. Having reluctantly given up his shoelaces, after a struggle, he had settled down quite philosophically to his plight and was sitting, fairly happily, in the cool of his surroundings and quite relieved to be out of the heat.

Maurice, like every other visitor to the festival, had duly paid his small fee and received his sampling glass. This was, however, unlike most other visitors, after a period of some confusion. Maurice's independence, whilst effective in a limited way, was restricted to environments and situations in which he felt comfortable and with which he was familiar. A crowded town square in France with stalls, some apparently giving away their fayre, and others not, was neither comfortable or familiar. He had not realised that he had actually bought the glass but thought that he was simply paying for its contents. He was further confused, when trying to pay for the next glass, that his money was refused and then, when he had finished, the stall holder insisted on him keeping the glass. Very impressed with this type of festival, and marvelling at the hospitality of the French, Maurice moved on.

The two glasses of wine had been quite enough in this hot sunshine and the piece of cheese he was now enjoying was delicious. He then continued on to the pizza stall where he pointed to several particularly nice-looking slices, gratefully accepted the plate from the generous stall-holder and wandered off without paying. The cries of "Monsieur! Monsieur!" were lost on Maurice, who, even without the general noise in the square, would not have heard much anyway. The next he knew he was being grabbed rather roughly from behind by some civic-minded bystander acting on behalf of the indignant pizza seller who, stuck behind his stall, could only shout with increasing indignation at the aged felon. Maurice, believing he was being mugged, swung out his arm in defence, and caught his assailant right in the eye with a piece of hot pepperoni. The young man, caught completely off balance, slipped

and fell to the ground. Maurice was then grabbed by several other passers-by who held onto him securely until the gendarmes in a blue van, lights flashing and siren wailing, arrived.

Had Maurice been French and been able to hear a little better it would not perhaps have taken too long to explain the source of the confusion. As it was, as far as he was concerned, he was apparently being arrested for being mugged! This did not go down too well and Granddad, survivor of a world war and several lesser confrontations, was not having any of it. The two gendarmes, hoping for a quiet day, were left with no alternative. This was not the first time that foreigners had overdone the wine sampling and then become stroppy. They unceremoniously bundled Maurice, kicking and screaming, into the back of the blue van, his panama hat slipping off and rolling away as they slammed the door behind him.

"Oh my God," cried Gloria. "It's Dad's hat!"

There lying in the gutter, bearing ample signs of having been trampled on, was, unmistakably, Maurice's Panama hat.

" Where the hell is he? What's happened to him?"

It was now seven o'clock; they had met up again in the main square after searching for him for two whole hours. There seemed to be only two places left to look for him, the hospital or the police station. The idea of looking in the hospital for her dad was too much for Gloria, and Eddie had seen a sign for the Gendarmerie not too far away so they decide to try there first.

"Ah, an 'old man," repeated the young police officer. "Oui, I sink we 'as 'im 'ere. Ah oui, 'is name is Maureese Carture, oui?"

"That's him," said Eddie, "Maurice Carter."

"Oh thank God for that," cried Gloria, collapsing into Maisie's arms. "Silly old bugger."

163

The Gendarme informed them, in a serious tone, that Maurice had been arrested for theft, common assault, assaulting a police officer and resisting arrest.

"Not too much then," said Eddie sarcastically.

Denis just gawped in admiration. "What a guy!" he thought. "What a guy!"

It took quite a bit of diplomatic negotiating, plus a generous donation to the 'Policeman's Benevolent Fund', before they managed to secure the release of the indignant Maurice. He still did not understand what had happened and assured the young gendarme that he would be going the British embassy and suing the whole force. Fortunately, they couldn't understand his shouts as he was being quickly bundled out by the others.

By the time they got back home, the excitement of the last few hours had taken away their appetites and the cheese and pate had become a bit sweaty in the bags. Still they managed to get through most of it before retiring. Jack, being a little more discerning, had insisted on a tin of spaghetti hoops before he was ready for bed.

Denis fell asleep trying to work out the French for "May I have a copy of the CCTV coverage of the Sainte Foy la Grande market square from yesterday please?"

Now that would be priceless.

Chapter Eleven

It was very important, whilst in the area, to explore some of the chateaux and towns which produced the wine for which the region was so famous. A visit to the town of St Emilion therefore was a must and it was not a great distance away.

As they approached the town built high on the hills of the Gironde and surrounded by acres of grapevines, Eddie read from a guidebook, "This golden village, one of the most beautiful in France, is famous throughout the world for its superb wines." His reading was greeted by the others with appropriate and dramatic 'ooohs and aghs'.

"St Emilion has many cafes where the famous wines of the area can be savoured in the shadows of its ancient buildings," Eddie continued.

"Whey heh!" drooled Denis. "Now you're talking."

The girls in the back were equally excited. Gloria, especially after her glorious triumph at the wine-tasting, was now viewing wine in a whole new light—she was, after all, as Eddie pointed out, "Almost a conwasseur."

Denis and Eddie would forever encourage this by mockingly deferring to her better judgement whenever they had a glass of wine; they could be quite irritating at times.

Missing from the party that day was Maurice who had been voluntarily confined to barracks after the excitement of St Foy. He was perfectly content to sit in the shade with a book, where he felt safe.

As the guidebook had stated there were indeed 'many cafes' where the wine of the region might be enjoyed, unfortunately most of them were fully occupied. However, a very accommodating waiter eventually invited them to sit in a large passageway, which led to the back entrance of a particularly attractive bistro. Surrounding the unevenly flagged floor of the passageway was a high stone wall that provided shade and cool from the hot sun. Draped in wisteria, clematis, and the odd geranium, it was quite beautiful.

The waiter disappeared inside before soon reappearing, dragging a table and returning for the chairs, tablecloth and cutlery. He had soon set up a place for them which was as good as anything inside; in fact, eating al fresco on yet another glorious day was perfect.

Tucking into a selection of cold meats and cheese, accompanied by a very reasonably priced St Emilion (after a nod of approval from Gloria), they wondered how it could get any better. Clare and Jack were perfectly happy sipping their Oranginas and enjoying the cheese and crusty French bread. Jack was assiduously avoiding the 'mouldy stuff' but he was packing everything else in and was reprimanded by his sister for eating too fast.

"Get lost," he said, spitting crumbs all over the table.

"Mum, tell him," pleaded Clare.

This usual spat was the only thing spoiling an otherwise idyllic scene and was easily resolved by sending them off in search of ice creams.

After enjoying the delights of the table, they spent the afternoon wandering around St Emilion, Maisie and Gloria exploring the shops whilst Denis and Eddie enjoyed the scenery and the views from the top of the town. They also ventured into a huge cellars, belonging to one of the châteaux, to check out the prices, but came out again having decided that they felt more at home checking out the cellars of the nearest *Intermarché*. Still they couldn't help but be impressed by the rows and rows of bottles representing all the wine producers in the area and the huge map on the wall indicating the locations of the various vineyards.

On their return from St Emilion, they called at a nearby château for a 'free' tour of their ancient caves. The young lady welcomed them and in very good, though heavily accented English, gave them the introductory spiel about the history of the area. She went into great detail concerning the unique nature of its soil, which produced such distinctive vines, and the various combinations of grape which made up a particular type of wine. Maisie and Gloria who had spent a couple of disappointing hours around the shops of St Emilion dominated by wine and wine-related products were beginning to lose concentration—in fact Gloria was literally nodding off. It didn't help that they were accompanied on the tour by a small group of French tourists for whom the nice young lady repeated the whole talk in their own language.

"Thank goodness there aren't any Japanese or Germans with us," whispered Eddie.

Denis was a bit put out that the French version of the commentary appeared to contain some humorous bits—though it could have had something to do with the way in which, by this point, Maisie and Gloria were definitely leaning against each other.

Carrying on from the first room, which housed the massive stainless steel containers in which the wine was coming to fruition, they began to descend far underground to the cavernous cellars of the château. These were reached by hundreds of steep stone steps leading down a narrow passageway, carved out of the rock. The air became very much colder and smelt musty and sweet. Jack who up to now had been completely unimpressed with the whole thing suddenly began to liven up—this was spooky. Clare couldn't believe how cold she was and found the whole thing, like her dad's 'ABC' tours, totally boring.

Deep in the bowels of the earth, their guide continued the talk, explaining how long the wine had to sit in its containers and how the wine down here was aged in oak casks. Denis nodded sagely as their host explained the intricacies of the various stages in the process.

"Fut de chêne," whispered Denis, knowledgeably.

"Denis!" rebuked Maisie.

"Fut de chêne," he repeated. "Aged in oak. Oh never mind."

"Fut de chêne, aged in oak," he whispered again to Eddie, pointing at the casks. Eddie just grinned.

"Bloody Philistines," he muttered under his breath, suddenly becoming aware that Mademoiselle had interrupted her commentary while she waited for Denis to finish his little distraction.

"Pardon, pardon," he said obsequiously, looking embarrassed.

At the end of this particular section of the tour they

were given time to have a wander around the gloomy caverns which Mademoiselle illuminated a little by turning on a couple of lights. This revealed the full extent of thousands upon thousands of bottles, which were stacked on their sides in racks all along the walls of the cave—some of them fairly recently, though many covered in dust and cobwebs had obviously been there for decades. In addition, alongside the long wooden racks, were large oak casks of various ages in which wine was slowly coming to maturity. It was after becoming stuck between two of these that Jack's hand was now firmly in the clutch of his sister, which did not go down too well with Jack.

Returning up the stairs at the end of the tour, they were taken as promised into the final room where they had the opportunity to sample some of the produce and, of course, make a purchase or two. Cue for more jokes at Gloria's expense asking her opinion of the various samples. Gloria, not a great red drinker, was not overly impressed with any of it and said so. Denis was repeating the routine he had adopted at the wine-tasting competition though this time he could afford to deliberate; whether he could afford to act on his deliberations was another matter.

"Oh this is nice," he said. "I'm definitely getting vanilla and a bit of pepper."

"Yuck!" said Jack.

"Dad," said Clare, mortified.

The others just stood trying to conceal their mirth. Was he serious?

"How much is this one?" he enquired casually.

"Er zat one is...let me see, trente euros. Certy euros."

"Ah right," responded Denis trying to appear unsurprised.

"Thirty euros. Ah hmm and this one, how much is this one?"

"Zis one is not quite so old and zis one is twenty-four euros. It's very nice."

"Oh yes, it is, very nice," agreed Denis, eagerly associating himself with this expert judgement.

As Denis continued his deliberations, he could see his dear wife's head shaking discreetly while her pretty little gob mouthed the words, "No, Denis."

Denis, caught between the rock of Maisie and the hard place of his pride, figured that Maisie would, as usual, forgive him eventually and bought the £18 bottle of wine.

Clutching firmly in his hand his bottle of *Chateau De Roques Puisseguin St Emilion*, Denis walked back out into the hot sunshine.

"£18 for a bottle of wine, bloody hell," he thought as they made their way back to the car.

"Well, good news, Clare, your Dad's feeling generous and we're going shopping tomorrow!" said Maisie, smiling at Denis.

Eddie, glancing down at the bottle, turned to Denis and enquired, "Fut de chène?"

"Don't you dare, Denis," warned Maisie.

The barbecue was what gave camping its special appeal—to eat *al fresco* seems such a natural way to conclude the day that it is strange that it was such a relatively recent addition to an English summer evening and to camping life. Where the tent is the cave, the barbecue is the roaring fire at the entrance, warding off wild animals whilst at the same time providing the means to cook the day's kill.

Whereas in the past the macho male walked ten miles home from his twelve-hour shift at the pit face, wolfed down a huge plate of raw tripe and onions followed by ten pints at the local pub before staggering home, kicking the cat, falling on the wife and getting up at five the next morning, today's macho man has a barbecue.

Denis and Eddie, who were real men, had real barbecues. They scoffed at gas-fired ones, they laughed in the face of ones with quick lighting briquettes: Denis' and Eddie's barbecues were true barometers of a man's masculinity. The thing was, though they never admitted it, for Denis and Eddie barbecue time was an opportunity for a modern man to state his identity. When there was more than one on the go at a time it was competition time.

Barbecuing was an activity full of mysterious and ancient male rituals. During barbecues territory was marked out, the dominant male's authority was established and the way the operator handled his equipment was clearly designed to attract a possible mate. Sadly for Denis and Eddie, this was all wasted on the girls. To Maisie and Gloria it was more a case of, "Oh good the blokes are doing the cooking again."

Still, this rather lukewarm appreciation of the ancient art didn't deter our heroes as they jealously guarded their gently stirring coals constantly on the lookout for suspicious-looking interlopers who were ready to interfere with such ignorant comments as, "That sausage is a tad black," or, "There's a lot of smoke, isn't there?" or, "Are you sure that it's still going?"

Serious exponents of the art of charcoal-induced cuisine had far more important matters to address to pay any attention to these inane remarks. How many firelighters to use? Obviously, the less the better. The speed at which the charcoals got going was crucial, and the moment when it was judged that 'all systems go' had been reached was indeed the moment of truth. It was this that decided whose barbie was ready for action first. Jumping the gun on this one was fatal because the food may then be contaminated with the flavour of smoke or fuel but even worse, if left too late, you may well lag behind a rival in producing the first edible specimen.

It was not, however, just how quickly things were ready to roll that was critical, the size of the inferno also played a part in the judging of the quality of a barbecue. Eddie, famous for the size of his pyre, constantly addressed, with one hand, the various items of food on the griddle, expertly turning them every few minutes—while in his spare hand was a glass which his assistant Gloria made sure, with some prompting, was always filled with wine.

Thus starting the operation as 'Eddie on fish', he usually ended up as 'Eddie on fire!' The scorch marks emblazoned (literally) on most of his face at the end of a successful cook-out were worn like a badge proclaiming membership of the 'real man's club'. Backing off from a blazing barbecue was not the stuff of real men. It would be to imply that the heat was excessive and that would be a sign of technical weakness. On one occasion, Denis's trousers had reached such a temperature that the heat transferring from his metal zip had melted the buttons on his boxer shorts. Unfortunately, he hadn't noticed until, on standing up, molten plastic hit flesh and—well—watering eyes were just not in it.

Despite the posturing and the third-degree burns, the

final result never failed to satisfy the primitive yearning for sustenance and everyone ended up well and truly pigged out. The drools of delight from everyone including Clare, apart from complaining that her burger was pink in the middle, meant that for Eddie and Denis honours were just about even.

Denis knew that it had been another successful night's barbecue when snuggling up to Maisie in bed later that night she had uttered those three magical words, "You stink, Denis."

"Goodnight, Maisie," sighed Denis, completely satisfied.

Chapter Twelve

Camping *au bord de la rivière* was a very enjoyable experience for everyone. Eddie managed to try out his skills on the River Isle, though the nearest he got to large fish was a visit to a local sturgeon farm.

The girls spent most of the time stretched out by the pool enjoying the continuing sunshine and, at the same time, 'keeping an eye on' Clare and Jack—Jack because of the dangers of the water in the pool and Clare because of the danger of the French boys in the pool. It was obvious to any casual observer that Maisie's concern was more about the latter. Gloria didn't help by telling her to relax, Clare was growing up and it was only natural.

"That's not natural what they're doing over there," retorted Maisie.

"Where?" said Gloria, suddenly sitting up. "Oh, I see what you mean, oh it's disgusting!"

Denis, having managed to find some bathers, which were neither skimpy or shorty, joined them a few times in the pool in between helping Eddie drown yet more worms and free tackle from overhanging branches which "weren't there a minute ago".

In between lazing around, enjoying the facilities of the

site, they enjoyed the odd trip out to local vineyards to replenish their supplies.

Maurice had seemingly had enough of the sunshine and was beginning to tire. He had never really recovered fully from his incarceration for theft and was just about ready to go home.

Though the days were passing swiftly, nobody had yet mentioned the fact that it was getting to the end of August and that it was nearly time to be heading back up north, towards Roscoff, ready for the ferry home. Still they had a few days left and there was time for an excursion out to find a bar-come-restaurant in one of the small villages nearby where they could enjoy some local French food; a holiday in France was never complete without a meal out.

On the way back from one of their little excursions, they called into a place on the edge of a village, which was little more than a few houses on a crossroad. It had been the 14 euro menu which had attracted them and, on entering, they were greeted in the usual welcoming manner by a large friendly lady who was only too happy to accommodate them that evening and would not of course charge fully for 'le petit'.

"She hasn't seen him eat!" thought Clare who was particularly sickened by the sight of Jack's affected angelic countenance.

There was nothing like a night out to lift the spirits, not that they needed lifting, but there was an added spring in the step as they prepared for their trip out for a meal. The girls began mid-afternoon and pulled out all the stops; they did not intend to allow this opportunity for a night out to pass them by without making the most of it. The boys also made a big effort—clean shirts which had not seen the light of day since leaving England were dragged out of suitcases and hung up to try and get as many creases out as possible. Shorts were discarded for long trousers, packed for the cold evenings, which had never really materialised. Eddie put on a pair of socks, which after nearly four weeks of sandals felt unusually cosy. Denis even had a shave which whilst they were on holiday usually came around about as often as Hayley's comet, only occurring when his face became intolerably itchy. Their whole corner of the campsite reeked of perfume and after-shave, the latter of which Denis had applied liberally to his badly cut face.

"Oh Denis, you look really young with a clean face," said Maisie. However, before Denis could get too excited she spoilt it by adding, "Shame about the bloody tissues."

Jack had reluctantly agreed to dress up too but only after being threatened with being left behind if he didn't. Clare had borrowed some of Gloria's make-up and was looking very grown up; she felt pleased with her appearance despite her brother's acerbic comments.

"You look like a racoon with that black round your eyes. Are you going to snog boys with that lipstick?"

"Get lost, sad boy!" she replied.

Maurice, emerging casually just before it was time to leave, very much looked the part. He had been spending his time in a fairly low key way over the previous few days but now feeling that he had served his sentence he was keen to be reintegrated into the community. Dressed immaculately in a shirt and tie, beige sports jacket, light trousers and of course his Panama, which Gloria had managed to reinstate to its former shape, he looked very much the proper English gentleman.

"Bloody hell," thought Denis. "He looks as if he's just stepped out of a five-star hotel rather than a tent!"

When they arrived the lady who had made them so welcome that afternoon was equally as friendly in the evening. They received some strange looks from the locals around the bar, dressed as they were in their 'going-out' clothes and Granddad sporting his newly recycled hat. Madame ushered them through to the back of the room which, though not separated completely from the bar, did feel like they were in the dining room.

"Er cinq repas, douze euros, s'il vous plaît," Denis said, slowly piecing together his sentence.

"Oui," replied Madame, reassuringly.

Denis was momentarily thrilled and then remembered that Maurice had turned his nose up at the fixed menu

"Er, what do you want, Maurice?"

"I don't know, what is there?" he replied, awkwardly.

"Why don't you look at the menu?" responded Denis, letting slip his irritation at Maurice for interrupting his flow when he was doing so well. He smiled wanly at Madame and tried to tell her that Granddad was just looking at the menu, which elicited a stream of conversation from her to which Denis was only able to say, "Oui, oui."

"You'll have to read it, Gloria," said Maurice. "I haven't got my glasses."

"Oh for goodness sake, Maurice," said an exasperated Denis.

"We should have left him at home," he added under his breath.

"Denis!" warned Maisie.

Gloria looked at the menu which might as well have been written in Chinese.

"What's that, Maise?" she asked, pointing at something which mentioned 'porc'.

"I don't know, what's that, Denis?"

"Er hmm it's, er, pork."

"Yeh, we know that, but what kind of pork?"

Madame intervened here; she took one look at the menu where Gloria was pointing and said, "Ah urmm, tres bien, gut, gut."

"What she say?" said Maurice cupping his ear. "What she say?"

"She said that the pork is really good," said Gloria, loudly.

"The pork's really good?" repeated Maurice.

"Yes, that's right. The pork is really good," confirmed Gloria, feeling that they were making progress.

"I'll have soup and a roll," said Maurice.

Denis, having by now lost most of his *joie de vivre* was left to pass this on to Madame who appearing to be completely unphased by the pantomime said, "Bon." And went off into the back before returning minutes later with bottles of water and three litre-bottles of house wine.

"Aperitif, Monsieur?"

"Deux bières, deux kias and deux oranginas, s'il vous plâit," said Eddie who was ready with the stock phrase, used whenever they ordered drinks.

"Oui, Monsieur."

"Oh well done, Eddie, you're so clever," said Gloria admiringly.

"What about Granddad?" asked Maisie. "Denis, order a drink for Granddad."

"Oh for goodness sake. Maurice, you're having a beer. Madame, une bière, s'il vous plâit, merci!"

"Oooh Denis," thought Maisie, quietly impressed with her husband's assertiveness.

The first course arrived in a big bowl in the middle of the table.

"I can't eat all that," said Maurice, almost before the bowl was on the table.

"It's not the soup," said Denis. "It's our first course."

"What is it?" enquired Clare.

"I don't know," said Eddie. "But I'm starving and it looks good."

"Er, qu'est-ce que c'est?" asked Denis as Madame was distributing the bowls and the serving spoon.

"Pomme de terre," she replied.

"Ah potato," said Denis looking around at the others confidently, sensing that he had regained the initiative.

"Yeh, we got that, Denis. Potato puree to be precise." Maisie always had to spoil things.

They soon saw off the puree and Jack in particular loved it, especially mopping it up with the bread.

Next was easy to identify.

"Cor, rainbow trout for the main course, yummy," said Eddie. "You can't go wrong with fish."

They all looked at him, and as he realised how comical this remark had been, Madame presented each of them with a beautiful pan-sized rainbow.

"These are just like the ones Peppi ate," laughed Clare.

"Wow," said Jack, as it was put in front of him.

"Ask her where my soup is," grumbled Maurice.

Maurice's soup duly arrived and he was very pleased with its rich vegetable composition, flavoured with herbs and spices. Its bright orange colour complemented the old-fashioned brown bowl it was served in. A nice granary roll would have completed it perfectly but Denis was not prepared to try and explain that to Madame and told Maurice that the French didn't do rolls.

"Well that was splendid," drooled Eddie, "but a few vegetables would have been nice. I wonder what's for pudding."

"Don't hold your breath, Eddie, I don't think that was the main course," said Gloria, as Madame came back in balancing a tray of something else. Into the middle of the table, she placed the thick slices of succulent looking ham, accompanied with pickled gherkins. Next to this, she placed a small decanter of olive oil. By this time Jack was beginning to flag—he had eaten a lot of bread with his potato puree and then some with his fish. The sight of the decanter, however, caught his eye, and he insisted on having some of the olive oil on yet more bread. The gherkins had no appeal and the ham he could live without but the olive oil looked intriguing.

As it transpired it had looked far more interesting than it tasted and he ended up leaving most of the oil-soaked bread on his plate, much to his sister's disgust. It was beginning to become apparent that this was another one of those eating places where the delivery of food and the serving of the guest were as much pleasure for the host as the meal was for the recipient.

They had in the past experienced meals out which had started with promise before disappointingly fizzling out— meals, which after a very impressive savoury course, had ended in disappointment.

One memorable meal in particular had been where Eddie had opted for the 'salade de fruits' and Denis for the 'gateau'. There was great hilarity especially from Eddie when Denis's imagined 'Black Forest' gateau with lashings of cream turned out to be a medium-sized slice of Madeira cake slapped on a small side plate. However, Eddie wasn't laughing for too long when his own small side plate arrived with a banana on it. Eating out in France, always an experience, was not always memorable for the right reasons, but tonight they seemed to have hit the jackpot.

The delicious slices of cooked ham were not the main course either. The main course was, as Madame had accurately described, the 'tres bien' porc. It was cooked in a rich creamy mushroom sauce and accompanied with the mandatory French fries. Jack's eyes lit up when he saw the chips his appetite, momentarily, coming back to life. By this juncture in the evening the three bottles of house red had, as soon as they were drained, been replaced by identical bottles and everyone was full of bonhomie. They had arrived at shortly after seven and it was now nearing eleven. They had munched their way through several baskets of bread, potato puree, rainbow trout, cooked ham and pickled gherkins finishing with pork in creamy mushroom sauce and that was just the savouries! Madame was now threatening them with a choice of desserts including 'crème caramel', an assortment of 'glaces', a 'flottante', 'gateau' or fresh fruit and before this she had appeared with a plate on which sat a large piece of soft cheese and a large piece of hard cheese. They were all beginning to buckle under the relentless assault but bravely they loosened their belts and continued, determined to reach the end of this, their latest gastronomic adventure. By the time they reached the end of the epic meal they were all fully laden with both food and drink.

"Digestif, Messiuers, Madames?" the hostess enquired mercilessly.

"Un cognac, s'il vous plâit," replied Denis.

"Me too," said Eddie.

"Ooh lovely, what should we have, Maise?" asked Gloria. "What about one of those pinot things."

"Oh good idea, Glo, they're lovely," responded Maisie, with a slight slur.

"And you, Maurice?" enquired Denis. "What is your pleasure?"

"I've had enough, thank you," he said firmly. "And so have you lot!"

"Deux cognac et deux pinots," Madame repeated in confirmation.

"Oui, parfait," confirmed Denis, his confidence high.

"Cigar, Eddie?" he said passing Eddie a large cigar which he had purchased especially for the occasion.

"Ay don't maind if ay do," said Eddie effecting an accent more in keeping with the nouveaux riches of the Empire than the capital's 'Old Kent Road'. They all laughed, except Clare, who couldn't see anything funny about her dad smoking cigars.

Denis, cognac in hand, was overcome with a feeling of mellowness; he was relaxed, at peace with the world and at one with his immediate surroundings. It had been a very good evening, the kind of experience that had reinforced all that he loved about 'la belle France'. Madame had been the perfect hostess, the food unbelievable, the tempo gently continental and the whole episode conducted in flawless (if somewhat limited) French.

Denis leant back in his chair, drew deeply on his cigar, inhaled the pungent smoke down into his lungs, and turned green. Unfortunately, Denis's smoking habit was punctuated with long periods of abstinence; in fact his last acquaintance with the old weed had probably been the previous Christmas. It was no real surprise then that the nicotine now being absorbed rapidly through this lungs and into his bloodstream, and combining with the large amounts of ethanol already there, were sending uncomfortable messages to both his brain and stomach. Why would Eddie not keep still and why had the meal he had so much enjoyed suddenly decided that it was not comfortable in its present resting place? Denis knew that he needed fresh air but wishing, as far as possible, to retain a look of control and normality, he very gradually levered himself up from his chair, carefully making his way across the room and through the bar, towards the door where there was a pinball machine. Leaning heavily against the machine, he took full advantage of the cool night air which wafted in through the door every time another customer left.

"Denis is ill," Maisie pointed out to Gloria.

"I know," replied Gloria. "And just look at Eddie trying to keep his eyes open, what a pair!"

Denis was soon joined by Clare and Jack who managed to guide him into putting the necessary coins in the machine and get the large silver balls rolling. By this time, Denis's co-ordination had completely deserted him and, as quickly as the balls appeared, they disappeared down the hole at the side. Denis, usually a fairly phlegmatic individual, was becoming increasingly agitated with the uncooperative machine and the gaudy flashing glass panel at the back was fair doing his head in.

"Calm down, Dad," pleaded Clare, as Denis began to rock and bang the machine. Jack, for whom his dad hadn't been so much fun for ages, was enthusiastically encouraging his dad's behaviour and joined in the onslaught. After waking Eddie up, Maisie and Gloria hurriedly sorted out the bill and managed to encourage Denis out of the door.

Madame was as gracious at their departure as she had been on their arrival and had been astounded at the amount of food which little Jack had packed away; it was always the best of compliments.

"Oh le petit, il mange bien! Au revoir, au revoir."

"Au revoir, Madame," Maurice returned, raising his hat.

It had been a great evening.

Back at the campsite Denis had been warned about not making too much noise, since the rest of the camp being asleep. But Denis's mind was preoccupied with other things. He was becoming aware of the need to keep as still as possible, so, while the others baled out, Denis sat there rigid, not daring to move.

"Are you getting out, Denis, or staying here all night?" enquired his wife.

"Just leave me a minute," replied Denis. "I'll be all right in a minute."

"Get out, Dad," said Clare. "Get out and go to bed."

"I will in a minute. You go, I'll be fine, jusht leave me a minute," he slurred.

While the others made their way off to the washrooms, Eddie fell straight into his bed with his clothes on. When they returned Denis was still sitting there stock still, in the knowledge that too much movement would result in the contents of his stomach ending up on the dashboard.

"He's still there, Mum," said Clare. "Dad, please get out and go to bed."

"Clare, just leave him, he'll be fine," said Maisie, trying to reassure her daughter.

"Just look at this pathetic lummox. You can get your bloody shoes off for a start, Eddie Lancaster!" Gloria screamed from the tent.

As the campsite returned to the silence of the night everybody, with the exception of Clare, settled down to sleep. Eventually at two in the morning after creeping out of the tent for one last attempt to get her Dad out of the car, she too gave up.

"Please, Dad, please come to bed—you'll get cold, please."

"Jusht leave me a minute. I'll be fine in a minute."

When he woke up at dawn the next morning wondering where he was, he was fine, well almost.

Chapter Thirteen

The next morning saw the sun rising on what was to be their last day on the campsite in Montpon, so it was spent washing pots, et cetera and generally making preparations for an early start for the journey back up north the next day. There was, however, to be one final night out on the campsite.

It had been Clare, whilst taking Jack up to a 'kids club' activity, who had first seen the poster advertising the 'Line Dancing and Lamb Roast Evening'. The girls were very excited about a line dancing evening, and eating out on the last night of camping thus avoiding having to dirty pans and dishes for washing up next morning seemed ideal. The men who had not been too excited at the time it was first suggested were even less enthusiastic after the previous evening's over-indulgence but they had been quite taken with the idea of a lamb roast and, still, they had all day to recover.

The mental picture conjured up by the idea of a lamb roast was that of a slowly turning spit draped by a succulently, meaty lamb, dripping its clear, juicy fat into a waiting receptacle to be later turned into sweet gravy. However, whereas the previous evening's meal had been unarguably a resounding hit, the lamb roast turned out to be a bit of a miss.

It was indeed a truism that the French were prepared to eat anything and this often translated itself into the availability of a huge variety of exciting and innovative fare. However, the flip side to this also meant that there were times when things were offered for consumption which in many other cultures and particularly English culture, would be steered well clear of, things for instance like *andouille*. At other times, there were things that should have been left in the field to see out their retirement in relative peace and quiet.

It is also universally accepted that words like pork, veal and beef are euphemistic terms used by the meat industry to protect the sensitivities of carnivores who perhaps wouldn't feel so comfortable eating a calf, or not wish to associate their dinner with a smelly pig, or a cow plastered with its own excrement.

In a slight twist but still very much a part of this convention, the word lamb is designed to conjure up pictures of a tender young thing gambolling in a field full of wild mint and new potatoes. Sadly, the lamb served up at the lamb roast had not been frolicking around the green fields of France for a very very long time, neither was it turning slowly on a spit.

When they had first arrived at the event it was clear that they were supposed to have brought their own cutlery, Eddie was quickly volunteered to go back and get it.

Inside the hall, the whole community of the campsite were gathered around two long tables which stretched from one end of the room to the other, while Monsieur Patron and his wife scuttled up and down between them distributing the wine, one plastic cup of red or white. Following the beverage, each person was presented with a plastic plate containing a generous slice of very course paté—not a favourite with the girls especially Clare, by whom it was greeted with a particularly heartfelt "Yuck!" Jack wasn't even prepared to touch it, the smell was the closest he was prepared to get. Maurice with perhaps less sensitive taste buds was quite content with it and happily received donations from the others so that by the time he had finished he was quite full, which was as it turned out, perhaps just as well. Denis and Eddie also quite enjoyed the paté but it was the large, succulent slices of roast lamb to which they were really looking forward.

"Not drinking tonight, lads?" asked Gloria feigning surprise. "It doesn't mean that we're not, Eddie, so you'd better go and get me and Maise a carafe of white wine."

Shortly after the paté had been given out, the music started with a young man with a voice not dissimilar to Frank Sinatra doing a rather impressive karaoke version of 'I Did It My Way' in English.

With the wine, which everybody had bought or brought to supplement the free cupful, beginning to take effect, the atmosphere soon lifted, and the evening began to take off. After coming to the end, for the time being, of a splendid repertoire, it was time for the singer to give way to the CD player while, at the same time, everyone was invited to form a line to receive their portion of the main event, the lamb roast.

The queue led down the side of the room and outside, into, and across the courtyard where from a row of several tables, pieces of lamb were being placed onto the flimsy plates. Denis and Eddie, of course, were balancing two plates each as their respective wives were, as usual, expecting to be waited on. After what seemed like an age, they arrived at the business end of the queue. The men distributing the meat were more than generous with the portions and both Eddie and Denis had difficulties in balancing the heavy weight of the meat onto their rather fragile plates. These became even less stable when the accompanying portion of haricot beans were added to each piece of meat.

In the semi-darkness of the courtyard, the lamb had looked quite promising but with the benefit of the light, it didn't seem quite so appetising. After the first mouthful, which took some getting off the bone, the true quality of the lamb was apparent. The sheep served up for the meal had obviously been acquired by Monsieur le Patron from a local haulage firm and had, whilst being transported on their final journey, been involved in a particularly gruesome motorway pile-up. With furtive glances followed by discreet comments, they all agreed that they had tasted better, in fact it was "bloody awful".

Looking around at their fellow campers expecting to see at least some consensus, they were surprised, but then not really, to see everybody chomping away happily. Whatever the animated conversations were about, it was nothing to do with condemning the food and after happily munching their way through the roast, what they wanted now was some more singing and some dancing. It was time to bring on the line dancers.

There was something a little bit incongruous about a French social evening featuring real French people dressed in Country and Western outfits. It offended Denis's sensibilities slightly, for whom line dancing, like synchronised swimming, was on his list of pointless activities. It was all proving to be a little bit monotonous, with lines, inevitably, of overdressed cowboys and cowgirls sporting silly grins, shuffling carefully, as if heavily sedated on Valium, in time to some noisy accompaniment sang in English with a heavy American drawl. It was all a bit tedious until a little man appeared and then things picked up.

Looking like a cross between Russ Tamblyn and Wayne Sleep, the little man whose name was Reuben was dressed in tight shorty-shorts and a tight vest which accentuated his diminutive but muscular body. Clare, who was facing the dancing, instantly recognised him as the little man who had latched on to her waist at the dancing display in Sainte Foy La Grande. After launching himself onto the dance floor and into one of the lines of dancers, he glanced over and catching sight of Clare, gave her a wave. Clare blushed and smiled. Gloria sitting on the other side of the table behind Clare and directly in Clare's line of site, waved back.

"Ooh look at him, Maise," she exclaimed. "And look at those muscles on his legs."

"Oh he seems to know you, Glo, how's that I wonder?"

"Well I think I remember seeing him around the campsite a couple of times," she replied, trying to sound nonchalant, but she was struggling.

"Well he seems to have remembered seeing you, look at him grinning over," said Maisie trying to sound impassive, but she was struggling even more.

With the appearance of this funny little man gyrating all around the dance floor, the line-dancing had taken on a sudden appeal to Denis and Eddie.

"Just look at Fred Astaire there, Denis, what a laugh," said Eddie.

"At least he's injected a little bit of life into the line-dancing," replied Denis. "And that's no mean feat."

All the while, the little man was responding to the favourable reaction that he was receiving from the well 'oiled' diners and, as more and more people joined him on the floor, the more his one-man dancing show relegated the official line-dancing display to the sidelines. As his gyrating increased, so too did the appreciation of the crowd who were by now banging the tables and stamping their feet in time to the country and western beat—even Maurice was clapping his hands. The more Reuben gyrated, the more they laughed and clapped.

"This is bloody funny, this is," said Denis, creased up at the sight and stamping his feet with the rest them.

"He's like one of those rubber men you see at circuses," remarked Eddie, with tears rolling down his cheeks as the little man performed seemingly impossible manoeuvres with his elastic legs.

"Just look at the way he can swivel his pelvis, Maise."

"I'm looking, I'm looking," said Maisie.

At that same moment Eddie noticed old swivel hips was looking over in their direction.

"Uh oh, he's looking at the gals for a dancing partner," warned Eddie. "Look out, Gloria."

The little man with the big ego was beckoning for someone to come and join him in the dancing but it was neither Gloria nor Maisie to whom he was addressing his request. It was Cinderella, on the near side of the table, who he had his attention and now he was coming to get her.

"Here he comes, Glo—who's first, you or me?" said Maisie.

Gloria wasn't open to such negotiations; she was determined who was going to be first. But before either of them had time to leap up, Reuben was on his way back to the dance floor, hand in hand with Clare.

To describe the grin on Denis's face as disappearing fast would be completely understating it. For Reuben, one minute some comical local character providing entertainment with his hilarious dancing routine, it had become, "What's that pervert doing with my daughter?"

Eddie face also had lost its beaming smile to be replaced with a slightly more internal one.

"Blimey," he thought.

The girls just sat there open-mouthed, their emotions a turmoil of shock, horror, humiliation, envy—you name it, they had it. For Gloria it was one rebuttal too far, for Reuben read Victoire, for Victoire read Olivier. "Little creep," thought Maisie.

The harmless snake hips had suddenly become a louche lizard and Denis was not going to sit there while he slithered all over his teenage daughter, who, to add insult to injury, seemed to be enjoying it!

Taking advantage of a middle-aged lady on her way to participate in the dancing, he grabbed her by the hand and clumsily joined in. Trying hopelessly to keep up with the rest of the dancing couples, Denis dragged his bemused partner around and around in vain as the tempo being set by Clare and her lithe partner prohibited any opportunity for Denis to catch up, let alone intervene. In fact, the more he tried, the more people he bumped into and it wasn't long before, in contrast to Clare's partner, who, with his exhibition of dancing had become the people's hero, Denis was swiftly becoming the villain.

Assuming that he was drunk, he was summarily dismissed by Madame. Abandoned by his partner, Denis continued for a while to dance around on his own in forlorn pursuit of his daughter. Clare was looking to her mum for rescue, not from swivel hips, but from her father!

"I don't believe this," she mouthed in the direction of Maisie.

"Do you want to sit down for a drink, Clare?" Denis enquired breathlessly, momentarily in speaking distance. "Do you want some cheese?"

Clare, blushing profusely, didn't have time to respond before she was once again whisked away.

Maisie, who had by now recovered form the initial shock and was slowly recovering her composure tried to call

Denis but the general hubbub and the noise of the music made any meaningful communication impossible. She eventually managed to catch his attention and in sync with a sudden lull in the music let out a very audible and non-negotiable, "Denis!"

Denis, realising the futility of both the chase and /or ignoring Maisie, scuttled back to his seat.

"She's sixteen, Denis, she's practically a woman. We're in a crowded room, full of people and she's dancing with someone nearly old enough to be her dad! Calm down, she's fine."

Denis knew Maisie was right of course, but it didn't help too much and he continued to monitor developments carefully. He needn't have worried; after one more circuit of the dance floor Reuben delivered Clare back to her seat, thanked her and graciously kissed her hand before departing.

"Hmm," thought Maisie and Gloria together, teeth clenched.

"Bloody Flash Harry," muttered Denis.

Clare sat rigid, not wishing to catch the eye of her mother or Gloria—she knew what they would be thinking. She was too ashamed to be seen associating with her father who had almost totally humiliated her—thank goodness he had never actually caught up! After this particular excitement, the rest of the evening was fairly low key. The dancing continued interspersed with the voice on the Karaoke and everyone, despite the standard of the catering, seemed to be having an excellent time; it was amazing how a drop of the nectar of the gods could be relied upon to lift the spirits.

Things were still in full swing when the gang decided

that it was time to head back to the canvas. They had been out quite late the night before and Denis and Eddie in particular were beginning to feel jaded. It had, overall, been a good night but, inevitably, their thoughts were returning to the next day's de-camping, the long journey northwards and the ferry home. The holiday was nearly over and, having come to the end of the final social event of the trip, they were all deep in thought as they made their way back from the bar. Mind you, there were one or two other reflections intruding on their thoughts, particularly for Denis and it would not have taken too much moonlight to reveal the cheeky little smile on the face of Clare.

Chapter Fourteen

After rising early the following day, in the comforting knowledge that they would be able to sleep on the journey, they were on the road before midday, which in camping terms constituted a pretty good start. As always, despite being caught out so many times before, they forgot about the midday closing regime practised by French retail outlets and therefore were too late to buy some provisions for the journey, so that would have to wait. They did not propose to complete the journey up to Roscoff in one hit and had intended to spend a night around the wonderfully famous Cognac area. But, sadly, they had decided to forego that experience and leave a day later in order to enjoy the 'magnifique' lamb roast. This resulted in them having at least to break the back of the journey in one day so as to be reasonably close to the ferry port to catch the boat the following afternoon.

The aim then was to get as far as just above Nantes, some two hundred miles north. Denis worked out that this was four hours plus an hour to allow for Eddie's navigating and a further hour for comfort breaks. That would take them to around six p.m., enough time to find an overnight campsite. Eddie's attention had been drawn to a place called Donges which was situated just off the main route from Nantes to La Baule. The idea of heading for a place called Dongeurs which he pronounced with a heavy roll of the 'r' amused Eddie and it wasn't long before he had irritated the others by constantly repeating it.

"Dongeurrrs, we're goin, to Dongeurrrrs."

"You're a noily prat, Denis," said Eddie reverting to his old favourite, "Yes, an oily prat."

"Shut up, Eddie," said Gloria half laughing, and he did, and promptly fell asleep.

It was a fairly straightforward route up through France picking up the D674 to Angouleme before heading west around Cognac and on to Saintes. From there the A10 took them straight up to Niort and then they headed north-west again, on the A83 towards Nantes. Having made good time by missing out the comfort breaks, since everyone was sleeping, Denis decided against continuing on the main motorway and so avoided having to negotiate the Nantes *peripherique*. Instead, he would give his old mate Eddie a little treat by taking him across the magnificent structure which was the bridge over the Loire around St Nazaire. This touching bit of altruism was later regretted when what always seems a short distance on a map of Europe turns out to be quite a detour. Shortly after leaving the motorway, near to Fotenay and heading towards La Roche the people in the back began to stir and demand the comfort breaks that Denis had avoided earlier.

"I should have bloody well known," he muttered. "It was all going too well!"

"Denis, you can hardly expect Granddad to sit for five hours without visiting the loo," chided Maisie, cleverly deflecting the blame.

"All right, all right," he said.

"Just don't blame me if we end up on some naff campsite or by the side of the road for the night."

"Yes we will, Denis."

"We can hardly help it if we haven't got hollow legs like you, Denis," added Gloria, which made Eddie laugh out loud, much to Denis's annoyance seeing that it was his damn bridge that had caused the diversion in the first place.

"I'm starving!" chipped in Clare for good measure.

"Me too," said Jack.

At least by the time that they got to the crossing of the River Loire with the sun setting behind it to the west, the huge structure, illuminated as it was in a brilliant sheen of light did look particularly resplendent. "You just watch where you're driving, Denis Wilson," said Maisie. "We want to look at the bridge, not drive off it!"

"What does it say about the campsite in the camping book, Eddie?" enquired Gloria.

Unfortunately, it had been the name Dongeurrs, rather than a description of any campsite, which had attracted Eddie. In fact, he had forgotten about this minor detail and kind of assumed that there would be one there.

"Er, do you know, I can't actually remember what the details were now but I'm sure that it is a good one," he said shuffling in his seat and offering up a little prayer—actually a big one.

They did eventually find a campsite and, though it was a municipal one, it was a very nice one. After setting up for the night they went off into the grand metropolis of Dongers to look for some food. It didn't take long before they found a pizza establishment, which they all enjoyed, except for Maurice who couldn't see why they were making such a fuss about cheese on toast. Mind you, despite his initial reservations, it didn't stop him from clearing his plate.

When they returned from eating, the campsite was very quiet and they wasted no time in checking out the ablutions and getting ready for bed. Though it was nearly midnight, there was enough moon to ensure that the sky was still fairly light. There was no breeze at all and, after the muggy heat of the day, the air was refreshingly cool. Although Denis had spent the day driving, or perhaps because of it, he didn't feel that tired and decided to sit outside the tent under the stars, reflecting on the events of the previous weeks. As usual it had been a mixture of the good, the bad and the ugly, which camping tended to be, but mostly good. It had never been boring and had been everything that he had anticipated and more. On top of that, it had all taken place in la belle France with its many fascinating quirks, its wonderful food and drink and its generally welcoming people. It was the freedom which camping offered that was so attractive, the nights like this, sitting out under the stars, at peace with one's surroundings, in perfect tranquillity...

"If you dive into bed and wake me up, Denis, I'll kill you," warned Maisie.

Denis was carefully sizing up the queues, anticipating which was moving the quickest and how soon they would be on board. The plan was that as soon as they were on the car deck, whoever could move the quickest, probably Clare, would go as quickly as possible into the bar lounge and bag seats for the others.

"I need the toilet," said Maurice from the back.

"We'll be on board in a minute, Dad," Gloria reassured him, but it was too late, the door was open and Maurice was off, just as the cars started to move forward.

"Bloody hell!" said Denis. "Bloody hell! Who took the bloody child lock off!?"

By the time Maurice reappeared, the people carrier had been pulled out of the queue and put into a holding area at the side. They were, in the end, just about the last to board. Taking Denis's plan literally, as soon as the car pulled to a halt, everyone went into evacuation mode and disappeared off into the body of the vessel—all except Denis who was still struggling to get everything they wanted out of the car. Denis's mood, never a particularly good one on the return leg of a journey to France, had not been helped by Maurice's prize performance and now, having to struggle on his own between tightly packed cars, was not helping at all. By the time he met up with the others, they were all settled around a table on the periphery of the bar and, when he returned, after forcing his way through the mêlée for a pint of Stella, Eddie was the only one still awake.

"Oh, welcome on board, Denis."

"Thanks for driving us all the way around France, Denis."

"We've had a wonderful time, Dad, thank you."

He sarcastically turned over in his mind the possible greetings which he might have been met with. Instead of the "Did you bring the sandwiches?" And "Sorry I didn't get you a drink, Denis, I only had enough for these in Euros."

"Wake up," said Gloria, shoving her friend in the ribs.

"I've got you a Southern Comfort and lemonade."

"Oh, what time is it?" yawned Maisie.

"It's 7.30, we're about half way."

"Where's Denis?" asked Maisie.

"Well he wasn't a very happy bunny and he said that he was going off to watch the in-voyage movie at the cinema." Gloria seemed to have a mischievous twinkle in her eye as she imparted this to Maisie.

"Oh yeh, what's he gone to see?" Maisie enquired innocently as she took a sip of her drink.

"*Shirley Valentine!*" replied Gloria.

The fellow passengers around about looked up with a start as Maisie's glass hit the table and smashed into pieces.

"Ooops," said Maisie.

Postscript

Denis, leaning heavily on the railings at the stern of the ship and staring out across the foaming wake of the *Duc de Normandie*, didn't hear Maisie creeping up behind him.

Sidling up sheepishly, she joined her husband as he watched the dancing white horses of the English channel provide some relief in the grey gloom which was quickly descending. The summer was drawing to a close and it was back to dreadful routine, general boredom, stress, strain, crap and Christmas!

"All right, love? How was the...film?" Maisie asked nervously.

"Oh, all right," responded Denis.

There was a pause.

Maisie, just about to launch into an explanation citing misunderstandings, that stupid Gloria, and anything else vaguely resembling a lifebelt, stopped as Denis continued.

"It was about some weird woman who went off to Greece and had some kind of mad fling with a local. Actually I fell asleep before the punch line."

"Oh. What was it called, Denis, do you remember?" enquired his wife, the relief beginning to emerge tentatively from its cover.

"Er, yeh that's the funny thing, *Shirley Valentine*. Do

you know, it's a bugger but I'm sure I've heard the title somewhere before but I can't for the life of me remember where. Ah well..."

"I love you, Denis Wilson," Maisie said as she wrapped both her arms around her husband giving him a big squeeze. "I love you."

"Ged off, yah big softy," Denis said laughing. "Look, there's the south coast of England just coming into view."